About the Author

Richard is a fantastic writer, an adventurer, and a very realistic part of this story (and writer of this short biography).

He knows that there are, from concrete experience, things that prowl the night that can hurt or even kill us.

He would also advise that Drarkland does exist, but under no circumstance should you try and visit it.

A Fistful of Fur

Lord Richard J Carberry

A Fistful of Fur

Olympia Publishers
London

www.olympiapublishers.com
OLYMPIA PAPERBACK EDITION

A CIP catalogue record for this title is
available from the British Library.

ISBN: 978-1-78830-239-5

This is a work of fiction.
Names, characters, places and incidents originate from the writer's
imagination. Any resemblance to actual persons, living or dead, is
purely coincidental.

First Published in 2018

Olympia Publishers
60 Cannon Street
London
EC4N 6NP
Printed in Great Britain

Dedication

I would like to dedicate this tale to my kids, my mates, and to Absolute 80's Radio Station, whose tunes kept me company on the nights when I sat and wrote it!

And to all the ladies who I love and love me… keep the adventure going girls!

Let Me Tell You a Story

Drarkland

West England 1885

The old man runs towards the tavern and behind him, the night follows. It follows like a hand reaching to grab him, to tear at him, to rip his flesh from his bones and devour him. Fear compels him to look back; he sees nothing, but senses something; something unholy, something that will suck the marrow from his bones and send his soul to damnation. Breathless and weak, he pushes on. The wind picks up, a soft distant howl teases him through the rustle of leaves, and he is sure he hears his name. He can see the tavern windows, illuminated, reassuring him like a beacon of salvation, and fuelling his hope of escape.

The inside of the tavern is silent. The few patrons that gather there are lost in their own thoughts. A shadow has returned once again to the village. The door suddenly bursts open and the silence is broken. A heartbeat too late, the old man screams as something grips him at the waist, his foot on the threshold of the tavern… a footstep too late!

The old man's life doesn't flash before him. As the grip tightens, he remembers the barn, the blood and the horror, flashbacks to the young lad's flailed flesh, half eaten, entrails spilled on the straw and the severed head found only today, discarded in the woods, no body to be found. How wrong the villagers had been, and how wrong they were now.

The old man tries to fight back. His attacker has him held low and is more powerful than he could ever be. They crash against the tavern floor.

Jacob Wilks, owner of the tavern, drops the tankard he polishes and looks on with shock. Ben Potts grabs his son, Jamie, and pulls him close, away from the danger. Chair legs scrape, terror grips their souls. The others melt into a melee of curses and screams as through the door the old man and his assailant loudly enter.

The old man is Martin Haines, the oldest worker at Drarkland Farm. Four days ago, the farm owner had taken on two young lads to help him out. Both seemed nice enough; tall and strong looking, though the dark haired one seemed to just stare from under his thick-set eyebrows. They would be useful for a couple of weeks, but it was only a few days later, the blond lad's body was found.

The morning sun was shining through the side of the barn, illuminating the terror on the farm owner's face, and the mutilated body of the young blond man lay propped up against the hay bales. The lad's head tilted back as the tendons of his throat hung loosely, the flesh torn out, and entrails spilled from the gaping hole in his chest. Below the waist, carnage. One leg was severed and missing, the other stripped to the bone and snapped. Haines noticed a mass of gore where the genitals should be and looking back to the poor lad's face, he was struck by his eyes... whatever those eyes had seen reflected something unholy and utterly terrifying. As the farm owner, Charlie, continued screaming, Haines turned and vomited.

The villagers agreed that the dark-haired lad must have done it and in a state of madness, used some type of weapon to murder his friend. That was until this evening, when the dark-haired boy's severed head had been found in the woods.

Haines breaks loose from the grip around his waist, and scrabbles forward on the rough wooden floor. His attacker begins to laugh! "You silly old goat." Brendon Turner, the butcher's eldest son, breaks from his laughter to point and insult Haines. He's drunk and dishevelled, and staggers back, crashing against the bar as he stands up.

"You bastard," Haines shouts. He too gets to his feet.

A chorus of insults agree. Wilks comes from behind the bar and grabs the drunken lout by the scruff of his coat. "What the blasted hell you playing at Brendon?" Spittle flies from Wilks' mouth, his large bald head red with temper.

Brendon Turner pulls himself free and starts to laugh again. "Playing a trick on that simpleton." He points at Haines. "Running down the hill like a scared girl so he was, all because there's a killer about... god man, the lunatic will be long gone by now." Turning to face Wilks he demands another drink. Before Wilks can reply, Haines stands and swings a blow, catching Turner's jaw who once again ends up on the floor.

Wilks and Ben Potts grab Haines. "In the woods, he's in the woods," shouts Haines, looking wildly at them.

Turner pushes himself up into a sitting position, rubs his face and spits blood.

"Who's in the woods?" asks Potts.

Haines struggles against their hold on him, "The other lad, the other one. He's in there."

Wilks looks at Potts, then towards the other villagers. "Let's get a group together, get into those woods and bring the fiend to justice." A silent nervous edge fills the tavern.

"No, you don't understand," says Haines, his eyes widening.

Turner begins to curse, and Wilks rubs his head. "What don't we understand, is he there or not?"

Haines pushes himself away from the two men and sits down. "Yes, he's in the woods... but only his head!" His words hang in the air. Looking towards the window he begins to shake. He can see the moon, swollen and full in its luminant majesty.

"Then they've both been killed?" Wilks asks, his voice slow and calm.

Haines nods. "Aye, and whatever it was that killed them is still out there and god knows how many others may die."

"Then it's back." A woman's voice comes from the back of the tavern. Norma Wilks steps out. "The curse has returned to Drarkland." She slowly walks towards the centre table.

"No, Norma, no." Wilks shakes his head at his wife.

She places her hands on the back of a chair and glances towards the door. "I knew when I heard how that young man was killed that it wasn't his friend. No man, not even a mad one can do that, and now the other one! No, it's happening. Again after all these years, its returned."

"I said no, Norma, enough." Wilks bangs his fist onto the table.

Haines steps forwards. "Listen to your wife, man! I saw the body in the barn, the head in the woods. It's back."

"Be quite, Haines," barks Wilks. The fire spits and everyone jumps and looks towards it. "For god's sake, woman, now look what you done. Got us all on edge, you have."

"This is stupid talk," Turner stands up, and staggers towards the tavern door. "Stupid talk for stupid folk. If I can't get a drink in here, then to the devil with you all. I'm off." he puts his hand on the latch.

"Brendon?"

He turns and looks at Wilks. "What?"

"Go straight home, you hear. May god be with you."

Brendon scoffs and walks out leaving the door open. One of the villagers quickly shuts it. The tavern once again falls into silence as the minutes pass.

"So? What do we do?" The question is asked by Jeff Barry, the general store keeper.

"I say we wait till the morning, have a village meeting. Enough has happened and been said tonight." Wilks looks around the tavern and heads nod in agreement.

Norma heads back towards the bar. "It's a start," she says, "but you've all got to accept that what attacked and killed those men was not human. Well, not fully anyhow."

"Norma, I said enough of that talk, it's just legends and myths. There's no such thing as a..." His sentence is cut short by a noise that freezes his blood to the bone and not just his but every man, woman and child in the village that night.

No one moves. No one breathes. All they can do is listen to the guttural howl that fills the night.

Long, piercing and hateful, the sound rides the autumn wind to haunt those who will never forget it.

The next morning Brendon Turner is silent forever. His throat has been torn out, and his body dumped in the village square.

Chapter One

South London, England

1985

Once upon a Monday night, at eleven pm or, in security officer lingo, twenty-three hundred hours, a bloke called Len Gordon walks from the entrance of the LMC bank and begins his hourly stint as an external security presence. Stepping into the night he lights a cigarette and blows smoke into the air. Looking up, he notices the moon and how full it is; it sits glowing in the darkness, clouds occasionally drifting past its face. Looking away, Len takes another drag and paces in a circle of boredom.

"Eight bloody hours to go," he mumbles as he walks around.

To be honest Len isn't much of a security deterrent. He's five feet five, slight of build with a panicky, sometimes squeaky voice which, you can gather, does not do much to strike fear in any would-be bad guy. His blond hair is gelled up, giving him the appearance that he's just seen a ghost, but in keeping with the latest fashion of this decade, it drapes towards his shoulders, therefore giving him, yes, you guessed it, a mullet cut. *If you can picture Lee Evans with a proper dodgy barnett, then pretty much you have Len.*

Len wants it to be the end of the week. In fact, he needs it more than anything. He's off Saturday and Sunday and then a week away in the West Country with his two pals. He wonders why his friend Chris has decided to choose such a place as a break for him and Ernie. A week in the country staying at a bed and breakfast! Still, a break is a break, and it was nice just to be away from the twelve-hour shifts as a security guard. Two weeks he'd been working for Able Security. Those two weeks had been the most boring of his life and even though he's off to the sticks and not the Med, he will be away from the constant dull atmosphere of this naff job.

Two weeks and three days earlier...

Gary Taylor walks into his local boozer. It's a Monday night and not much is happening in the Wayward Mans Rest.

Wearing his brand-new Nike blue swish trainers, faded split-bottomed Loise jeans and black Lyle and Scott jumper, he heads towards the bar, his gallon of Drakkar aftershave reaching it long before he does. Tracy Loosely, the barmaid, is leaning across the counter studying her nails, her breasts battle to stay in her pink flamingo deco top. Girls on film by Duran Duran plays on the juke box. She looks up and smiles, masticating all the time on her gum. "Alright Gary?" she asks in that good old saff London voice. She fancies Gary, he's got a nice face; square jawed with dark stubble, deep brown eyes and dark brown short spikey hair... shame he's got a bird, she thinks.

Gary smiles and pulls out his wallet. The local wide boy whips out a tenner and slams it on the bar. "Yeah, I'm alright, sweetheart. Pint of lager for me, whatever your having." His smile widens, and he gazes towards the obvious, "and whatever your mates want too." He breaks into a dirty laugh.

Tracy, pulling her top up, grins. "Sauce! I'll have a vodka orange in the pot for later thanks. You wanna try one of these new Belgium beers?" she enquires as she snatches his note.

Gary looks at the pumps and pulls a face. "Nah, I'll stick with the British ones, pint of Carlsberg, babe."

Looking around he spots Fatty Jock sitting on his own, nursing a scotch and reading the paper. He's called Fatty Jock for two good reasons; one, he's fat and two, he's Scottish. Tracy gives him his change and he smiles and once again takes time to look upon the struggle she has going on inside her top.

He takes his change with his drink and heads towards the Scotsman. He bids him "Allo" and sits down at the table. Fatty Jock looks and nods. "I've heard you need security guards for your site at the bank?"

Fatty Jock looks at him questionably. "Aye...so?"

"Well, I'm worried if you don't fill them positions, things could easily go missing; the crime rate round here is going through the roof."

"Well don't be worried, I've got some recruits coming in for training tomorrow."

"Yeah, but it's them recruits I'm worried about...I mean, who are they? I'll tell you who, work-shy drop-outs that'av been forced to leave the dole. They don't want to work, mate! They won't care about keeping their mince pies open. No son, they will be Bo-Peep before you can finish ya bedtime story. You need someone who's alert, keen and fearless! Someone who can be trusted and relied upon! And with this potential member of your security team there comes a very attractive chance of money-making opportunities."

Fatty Jock leans forward and stares at Gary, trying to think what he could possibly be angling at. Within moments it becomes apparent; the recently unemployed Len Gordon has just been plucked from the dole and given the opportunity to become a security officer at Able Security Services.

Gary returns to the bar, happy. Fatty Jock sits back in his chair, happy… and Len, well at least it's a job, or as it turns out, two jobs.

Len flicks his cigarette, he watches the sparks fly as it hits the curb and bounces onto the pavement. Looking at his watch he frowns as he has another fifty minutes until he's relieved by another officer and then it's his break, or it would be, if he hadn't had to go into the bank's equipment room. The equipment room, home to various pieces of kit including a double-decker video recorder.

A double-decker video recorder is a piece of kit that can record one video to another, hence the opportunity to make multiple video films. The photocopier, another piece of kit that can photocopy things… things such as labels that can be copied, cut and stuck on video cassettes to indicate what films are being flogged around the pubs, clubs and cafes in south London, making a considerable amount of cash. The cash, split between

Fatty Jock and Gary Taylor who sits back and does sweet FA while Len, Len, does all the graft.

Lens thoughts are interrupted as his radio crackles and Senior Officer McLash (Fatty Jock) makes an announcement from his security control room.

"S/O Gordon… over." (*Genuine radio protocol*)

"Receiving… over."

"I've picked up some movement at the rear of the bank in the refuse area. Could you please investigate… over."

It would be only fair to point out that not only is Len small for a security guard but he's pretty much a nervous wreck too. Len curses the fat Scotsman and begins his journey to the refuse area where all the big bins and rubbish is stored.

An uneasy silence seems to fill the night, the moon seems to grow unnaturally in size and something moves between the boxes. Amongst the bins and black sacks, it lopes and then settles, crouched. It hides, watches and waits.

Len reaches the rear of the bank. He feels uneasy. He's swallowing hard and farts. He walks slowly towards the refuse area. He tells himself it must be a rat or fox that has run among the bins.

How wrong he is!

Len stands now in front of the rubbish, reluctant to go any further. He looks around for any sign of movement, but all is still. "Control from S/O Gordon, all is OK… over." He sighs relief and turns to walk away. His radio crackles… shit!

"S/O Gordon, you need to proceed into the actual rubbish and check… over."

Shit, shit, shit. His nerves begin to tingle the way they do when he knows something bad is going to happen. If it wasn't for him needing to save some money for his son, Len Jnr, he'd return to control and tell them to stick the job, but for once, he must man up and think of his kid. And with that, Len turns and heads into the rubbish.

It sees Len and a grin peels its lips apart, muscles tensing, eyes fixed as its prey moves closer. The noise that fills the night and Len's head, is something made by neither beast or man but something in-between. The sacks of rubbish part and explode as the dark shape leaps forward, hands clawed, stretched out, reaching to grab him…to tear at him.

Len falls backwards as the force of the twisted figure lands upon him. Len notices the moon has turned red. He lands on top of the sacks, the wind rushes from him, he waits to die… the moon red, blood red…The moon is not red or blood red, the street light above the refuse area is though! The clawed hands are slapping him across the face, and he can hear howling.

The howling has been replaced by laughter and as Len looks up, the twisted figure grins… Gary Taylor winks and stands up. It takes Len's mind a moment to process what has happened. Gary is laughing and pointing at Len, then his radio crackles. The voice of Fatty Jock bellows, "HAHAAA! Len, ya wee numpty, get up."

Len stays still for a moment and then slowly, starts to make his way to his feet (*a comical piece of lettuce rests on his shoulder as you would expect in such a scene*).

"Lenny, mate, I couldn't resist! Your boat was a picture! Me and Fatty Jock thought we would prank ya. We got it on video and everything. One day this will make you famous, son, you wait and see," he cackles and brushes himself down. "You done them vids yet?"

Len begins to feel himself boil. He looks at his so-called Jack the lad mate and starts to become angrier and angrier. The prey becomes the predator. Losing his shit completely Len throws, in temper, his walkie-talkie at Gary. It's a direct hit in the man jewels, and once again howling fills the night.

Chapter Two

Many years ago, a film called 'Carry on Screaming' was created and it was shown at the cinema and on television. If you remember it, picture the monster named 'Oddbod'. If you're too young, or have never seen or heard of it, please take the time to go Google it and the mentioned beast!

...OK, for those that popped off to Google, welcome back. Now you know what one of the main stars of this tale looks like, let me introduce you all to Ernie Smith!

Ernie is in his bedroom and he gets ready for a good night's sleep. Ernie is currently talking to us through his own thoughts.

"Live fast, die young, that's my moto! If your gonna' cruise, cruise fast! To be fair, my steel horse is me mum's old moped but...but cruise on it I do. I cruised past some chicks today, cruised past them as they peddled their bicycles. Obviously, they fancied me 'cause when they overtook me, they were smiling and giggling. Some birds don't really say much. I think they see me as out of their league; that's probably why I ain't got a girlfriend."

Ernie sneezes, and snot nests in the bum fluff beneath his nose. Oh, how irony can be so mean. His entire body is covered in thick black hair, his eyebrow is just a unibrow but for some cruel reason he can't grow a proper thick moustache. Ernie wipes at the snot.

"Some women might not like the danger that a Hells Angel like me brings with him. To be fair, most people give me a wide birth." Ernie breaks wind; a foul stench fills his room.

"Fear me, they do. Don't mess with me six feet four of muscle." Ernie is six feet four and with his clubbed boots, he reaches even greater heights but it's fair to say it's not muscle. He's just a tall bloke with a bit of a paunch.

Ernie strips down to his underwear. It's hard to say which has the most stains, his vest or Y-fronts, but if you were mad enough to look closely enough, you'd realise they were once both white.

"Here I lay in my ghetto shack, my midnight-black hair pushed from my face, well, not so much now that me mum accidently gave me a blunt fringe. I say ghetto shack; my parents bought the three-bedroom semi off the council a few years back. But here I lay, another day another dollar and back in battle tomorrow."

Ernie closes his eyes; his digital display clock indicates it's twenty past nine. He thinks of work at the general store with his friend and boss, Chris. Tomorrow is staff training day, so he'll go in early. Ernie farts again and chuckles at its loudness. Next month he'll be thirty-four. He starts to think about his birthday and drifts off.

Hours later and with morning arriving, Ernie's senses awaken him before the alarm… bacon, his mum is making bacon. He rises from his pit, eyes closed but his nose is like a bacon radar. He leaves his room and starts to descend the stairs. The smell of bacon fills his nose, and a few more stains mark his pants.

Tuesday morning, Chris Murren has woken pretty much the same time as his friend, and employee, Ernie.

Turning off the alarm, he sits up and swings his legs over the side of his double bed... a bed that he often thinks will never be filled by two. Standing up he stretches, his belly momentarily raises above his pants and then, releasing a yawn, it flops back down and covers them. Scratching his head, he makes his way to the bathroom. Looking in the mirror, he examines his reflection, and thinks back on last night's comments in the pub.

"Don't know what Gary's on about, I look nothing like a guinea pig with a bowl haircut!"

He brushes his teeth, combs his brown hair and has a pee.

Chris does look a bit like a guinea pig and he does have a bowl wedge-type haircut. He also has a nice three-bedroomed detached home in the better part of town... much better than where his friends live, and a nice little general store. Today is staff training day, and Chris can train his staff, all one of them, and pass on his wisdom.

Chris and Ernie were at school together, as were Gary, Len and the yet to be introduced, Tommy Harris, and out of them all, Chris had made the most of things. Chris was always the one to introduce his friends to new ideas, to different cultures, to understand the finer things in life... as you've read for a better part so far, it has never really worked.

Still, where there's life.

Chris thinks of the trip that he, Ernie and Len are heading off on next Monday. It's summertime and what better way to spend it than in the West Country. Clear skies, fields of green, miles away from the smoke fumes of London... and away from Gary and Tommy!

Chris is dressed and ready to leave as he does he puts on his last garment, his long brown work coat with the special badge, the special badge that says, Chris Murren - Manager.

By the time Chris arrives at the store, Ernie is already there. He looms in the doorway, probing his nostril with his index finger. Chris bids him good morning; Ernie grunts and continues to pick his nose. "Could you not do that, Ernie. I don't want customers to see the real you." Chris unlocks the shop's front door and rushes in to turn off the security alarm.

Ernie wipes his finger on his trouser leg and follows inside. "If they saw the real me, the women would fall at my feet, and the men would flee in fear."

Turning from the alarm panel Chris turns to face him. "Speaking of feet, you're on your own in the B&B next week. Len and I are sharing a room, you got a room all to yourself."

Ernie frowns. "What's that got to do with feet?"

"Because yours smell hideous, and the sight of you in your underwear provokes insanity."

Ernie shrugs. "Suits me, be better on me own anyway...for when I pull a sort."

"Let me tell you something," Chris snaps, "I've been looking forward to this holiday for ages, to relax and take in nature. Gary and Tommy aren't invited for very good reasons, so don't you be creating any of the mayhem that they normally induce on our trips away." Ernie pulls a face and heads towards the back room. "Where you are going? I'm doing staff training now."

"Taking a dump."

Chris sits at the counter, shaking his head he wonders why he didn't just invite only Len.

Across town Len has finished his shift. He sits in his flat, and from his bedroom wardrobe he gently lifts out what at first glance, looks like a metallic anthropoid, but on closer inspection it becomes a camera, a very old camera. Len's latest hobby.

He came across it at a jumble sale a few years back when he was with his wife, Jenny, but since the camera had ended up in the loft of his previous home, and now that he and Jenny had separated, it had been dropped off by her twat of a boyfriend, Keith. With Jenny gone, and the camera at large Len had decided to fix it, to make it work, to give it a chance to be like it was many years ago.

So instead of bed, Len begins work on the object in question. He turns on the radio, hums to Bananarama and thinks of his eleven-year-old son, Len Jnr… hopefully, it won't be a cruel summer leaving him here on his own!

Ernie has come out of the karzie, he sits in a chair and listens to Chris as he spouts on about approaching a customer. "So, you see, Ernie, if I say to a customer 'do you *need* any help?' they can say no…but if I ask, 'how *can* I help?' well, they can't say no."

"Why?" asks Ernie.

"Because it doesn't make sense. You can't say no to '*how can I help you?*' but you can say no to 'do you need any help?' You see, once you have the customer engaged in conversation, you stand more of a chance of selling them something."

Ernie slurps his tea and takes another biscuit out of the packet.

Chris shakes his head and stands him up. "Look, let's role play, I'll be me, and you be the customer."

Ernie shoves the biscuit in his mouth and walks to the door. Turning, he saunters into the shop pretending to be a customer. "Morning sir, do you need any help?" Chris beams.

"Yes, I want to buy set of knuckle dusters as I'm a Hells Angel and want to rumble." Some of his biscuit crumbs fly from his mouth and land on Chris's chest.

"What was that?" Chris asks angrily, brushing himself down.

"I'm doing what you said, I'm role playing."

Chris flaps his hands up in the air. "Not like that, you fool. You're supposed to just say NO."

Ernie looks confused... "But why?"

"Because, jelly brain, it's part of the point I'm trying to make."

Chris shoves Ernie and tells him to do it again. Ernie once again walks into the shop pretending to be a customer.

"Morning, do you need any help?" Chris asks, not so politely as before.

"No," Ernie replies.

A smile appears on Chris's face. "Right now, go back and walk in again."

Ambling towards the door Ernie does as he's told, and once again walks into the shop pretending to be a customer.

"Good morning, sir, and how can I help?"

"You can help by telling your staff to be politer."

Chris looks confused. "Sorry?"

"I was here a moment ago, and your staff member abruptly asked if I needed any help. He never once referred to me as sir and was loud in his manner."

Chris looks on in disbelief but before he can retort, there's a bang on the shop door. They both look over. It's Gary. Ernie lets him in. Before Gary can speak, Chris jumps forward. "Good morning, sir, and how can I help you?" Chris looks at Ernie, smiles, and indicates to Gary.

"No," Gary replies. Chris walks off mumbling under his breath, his face flushed red. Ernie grins, and in the distance Chris screams.

Keith, Jenny's twat boyfriend, has been with her now for a year. He is the manager of the local furniture store and treats Len like he treats his staff, nasty and rudely. He always seems to plan family trips with Jenny and Len Jnr, when it is Len's time to see his son. Little Len didn't see the nastiness Keith was doing, but Len did and if he complained, Keith managed to twist things so he was in the right, and Len in the wrong! Jenny would stand by Keith, blindly, and he would be the one to lose out. Putting such things from his mind, Len studied the book he had from the library. It was all about the camera he was restoring. All he needed now was the powder to create the flash and bingo, it would be ready for their holiday.

"What's up with Chris?" Gary asks Ernie.

"Dunno, must be his time of month."

They both laugh.

"Listen, Ernie, last night I got another batch of videotapes sorted from Len. Has your old fella got any more cases in his lock up?"

Ernie nods. "Yeah, same price as before?"

Gary agrees and makes his way to the door. "OK, mate, I'll see you for them later." He shouts goodbye to Chris who responds with an obscenity. An old lady that has just entered Murren's general store shockingly blushes and walks out again.

Gary climbs back in his van and looks at his watch; he'll pick Tommy up and go to the café but first there's some more business to be done. He'll grab Tommy and drive towards the route of a girl known as Primrose Lil!

Primrose Lily descends the stairs and walks into the kitchen.

Her father sits studying the *Times*, her mother stands next to the sink, fag in one hand the *Sun* newspaper in the other.

"Hello (ello), my darling. You look lovely," her mum's broad London accent welcomes her good morning.

"Morning Primrose," her dad mumbles in a more educated brogue.

"You want some breakfast, love?" her mum asks. Chucking the cigarette in the sink, she extinguishes it by running the tap.

"I'm fine thanks, Mum, piece of this toast will do," she politely answers as she lifts the lime-covered bit of burnt bread, examines it and drops it back on the plate.

"Very wise, Primrose," her father stands up folding the newspaper and placing it on the table. "Very wise indeed. So far this morning, not only has your dear mother burnt the toast, bacon and sausages, she's also burnt my tie."

Dolly, the mum, sticks her fingers up. Hugo, the father, clasps them together, chuckles and kisses her on the lips.

Primrose giggles.

"How did you burn father's tie?"

"I was ironing it and watching the telly at the same time; some bird named Dizzie Lizzie was on there doing aerobics and she distracted me."

"It's a good job I have many others," he winks, lovingly pats his wife on the hip and leaves to retrieve one.

"Your dad still makes me go all weak at the knees when he wears a suit."

"Mum, Daddy's a lawyer, he virtually lives in a suit."

"I know," Dolly sighs, "That's why I always walk funny."

As Dolly loudly cackles, Primrose smiles and heads towards the full-length mirror in the hallway.

She examines her look.

Shoes... polished to a gleaming shine.

Charcoal grey skirt and racing green blazer... pressed and sharp.

Tie, straight and un-burnt.

Hair... up and in two side pony tails.

All in all, Primrose Lil is a poster girl for the posh grammar school she attends.

"Right, Mummy, I'm off."

Dolly speedily shuffles to where she stands, holding both her cheeks in hands adorned with rings. She kisses the head of Primrose and bids her farewell.

"Have a great day at school, poppet," her father shouts from somewhere upstairs. "And don't get into any trouble."

"Oh, Daddy," Primrose laughs and shakes her head. Stepping out into the day she closes the door to her large, detached house in a very good part of town and walks down the concrete steps onto the pavement.

Satchel over her shoulder, chin up and back straight, the thirteen-year-old strides to school.

The rough kids from the Brunt Hill Secondary congregate around the top of the lane that Primrose must use in order to cross into Hayfields Park.

She can hear their course language and bad grammar and today they seem rowdier than usual.

As she nears, she notices a large, thick-set boy older than her pushing a slight, smaller boy around till eventually the poor kid falls over.

Len Gordon Jnr lays on the pavement and, with frightened eyes, looks up at Brunt Hills biggest bully, Andy Towers.

"I told you, ya little tosser! I want a pound a day protection money or else."

He bends down and grabs Len Jnr by the tie, twisting it round his large hand. Len Jnr feels it tighten; he starts to choke.

"Len Jnr!"

The sudden interruption into his demise comes from a smartly-dressed girl that pushes her way through the crowd to stand with patient shoes next to his head.

Andy Towers stops twisting the tie and glares towards her. Len Jnr smiles.

"Primrose Lil," he rasps.

Primrose places her satchel on the floor and marches towards Towers.

"This will not do! Len Jnr your father will go mad if you damage your clothes. Seriously, you should not be brawling with undesirables in the street."

She removes the hand from his tie and clucks. Helping Len Jnr up, she shakes her head and pats him down. Len gazes into the beautiful face of Primrose Lily, his secret crush since, well, since always!

Towers stands dumbfounded, then realising what the girl has done, flares into a rage of obscenities and violent threats.

The white transit van slows down; the driver and his friend look towards the gang of kids.

As Towers grabs one of Primrose's pony tails, the driver smiles and shakes his head. His companion, a blond, thick-set man with glasses, growls.

"I'm going over there."

"Stay put and watch."

"There's a poor girl about to get the granny knocked out of her by some ginger lump... and you want to watch!"

Gary turns to face Tommy Harris and smiles.

"That ain't no poor girl, son... that's Primrose!"

Tommy leans forward.

"Oh yeah, bleedin' hell. I need stronger bins mate."

The pain he feels as her hand grabs his man jewels is sickening. Instantly, he lets her hair go and slowly he falls to his knees as she too releases her grip.

She stands above the large red-headed boy as he kneels before her, groaning.

"See this ginger pig-eyed cowson," her voice is loud, and her accent has taken a turn from posh to... well, not so posh!

"He has put his hands (ands) on the wrong person! Let me tell you all... and especially you, ya fat bastard." She grabs a handful of his hair and yanks his head to look at her. "Anyone touches my mate Len and they get this."

Letting go of his barnet, she slams her knee into his face. There's an explosion of blood from his lip and he falls back, squealing.

The group all nod and speedily depart. Primrose lowers herself and with the sweetest of smiles and voices, informs Andy Towers she will be collecting from his person, two pound a day for the rest of the next term (this was their last week before the summer holidays) ...moneys to be paid to Len at school. Len to forward all cash to her when summoned.

"Thanks, Primrose," Len Jnr responds, trying to kiss her cheek. Primrose recalls in horror.

"Errr! Get of me, ya little git! Now bugger off to school before you're late."

Making his departure, she picks up her satchel and fishes about until she finds the single cigarette that she chawed from her mum's box.

"Ah, bollocks. I aint got a light! Oi, ?Ginge, you got a light?"

Andy groans and shakes his head from where he still lays.

"N-n-no... sorry."

"Bloody useless, you!" She spots the white transit across the road and waves at the driver.

"Primrose Lil," Gary welcomes her as she stands next to the door of his van.

"Uncle Gazza," she replies..."Alright, fat boy," she greets Tommy.

Tommy sighs, "I'm not fat, I'm muscular, Primrose."

She laughs, flicks her pony tails and sticks the cigarette back in her gob.

"Any of you two losers got a light?"

Gary fires up her cigarette and chuckles.

"Don't tell mum, OK!" she warns, blowing out a stream of smoke and slinging her satchel over her shoulder.

"Like I'm gonna tell my sister I've given her daughter, my niece, a light for a fag," Gary laughs. "You got the list of contacts?"

"You got the readies?"

As Gary hands over the money to Primrose, she hands to him a piece of paper with all the names and numbers of people interested in his dodgy videos.

"Was nice doing business with you, Primrose."

"TTFN, uncle."

Primrose Lily smiles sweetly once again, turns and wiggles her fingers goodbye. She trots past the still fallen Andy, pauses to look at him then continues on her way to St Mary's... a school for bright, gifted and charming young ladies.

Chapter Three

Gary parks his van outside his flat and carries the cassette boxes inside. Entering the flat he can hear voices. He knows he's late, but business is business. He is greeted with a cold stare by his girlfriend (and Len's younger sister), Becky Gordon, and sitting on the sofa, are her and Len's parents.

OK, a quick update on the situation. Gary has been going out with Len's younger sister, Becky. She is two years younger than Len. Becky moved in with Gary three months ago and though he's not particularly happy about living with a girl, Gary agrees as Becky is incredibly fit, and for some reason, loves him. Having known Len most of his life, his parents are aware of Gary Taylor and his dodgy ways. Having agreed to get off on a better foot, her parents have been invited for a sophisticated dinner evening at Gary's flat tonight. It's a chance to convince them he's not the wheeling dealing wide boy everyone portrays him to be, but a mature and hardworking man quite capable of taking care of their daughter.

"Evening," Gary greets them with a smile, and dumps the boxes in the corner. "Something smells good."

The evening is a success. Becky's parents are so charmed by him, they invite them over to a lake house they have recently purchased near the Broads. Once there Gary lays in a small boat whilst Becky gently rows them along, telling him how wonderful he's been, Gary says nothing, and just lays there letting the sun warm him. A banging noise can suddenly be heard in the distance. He tries to ignore it, but it becomes louder and louder. Suddenly it was like it had seeped into his head. Pain flashing behind his eyes, he sits up in the boat…he sits up in his bed! Just a dream.

"Oh. You're awake, you 'orrible bastard."

The pain is savage, and Becky's shouting and banging aren't helping. "My head… what has happened to my head and what's up with you?"

Becky slams a drawer closed, and shoves underwear in an open suitcase. "What's up with me? You were so out your nut last night, you can't even remember."

Gary rubs his face and scratches his stubbly chin. "We played Trivial Pursuit with your parents, had a few drinks, had a few laughs and they left!"

Becky stops what she is doing and leans on the bed. She's angry as hell but she was still a blinding looking bird, he thought. "You came in late with a load of boxes for your pirate porn movies. You got pissed at the dinner table and kept referring to my mum as Popeye."

"Was just a joke!"

"A joke! You insensitive asshole; she's still recovering from an eye operation."

"Sorry."

"You used foul language," she begins counting with her fingers. "You told them how you scared the shit out of Len at work the other night. You called my Dad 'Curly' and slapped his bald head. Then in the middle of Trivial Pursuit you accused them of cheating and kicked the board over. Then you passed out with your head buried in the chair, and your trousers and shorts around your ankles." She stops counting and continues to pack her belongings.

Gary sits, rubs his face and tries to remember. "To be fair, I think your old fella was blaggin' some of the answers on Tri..." He is cut short as Becky launches a trainer at his head; it misses by inches. "Babe, please let's not fight, let's talk... I'll take your parents out to lunch later."

Becky grabs her suitcase and walks to the bedroom door. "I'm going to stay with Jane for a while, until I've sorted my head out."

Gary flops back in the bed. "Sorry," he mumbles but Becky is gone. The front door slams. Gary winces and closes his eyes.

Tommy Harris pretends to be asleep whilst his girlfriend, Jane, speaks on the phone next to the bedside table. He is fighting with every fibre in his body not to laugh when he hears something about bare arse in the air and dribbling... what has his best mate, Gary, done now!

Jane reassures Becky that she can stay 'as long as she wants' and that's when he stops chuckling inside and sits bolt upright in the bed. Jane gets up and leaves the bedroom. When she comes back Tommy is sitting with his arms crossed and glasses on. Jane smiles; she likes the way Tommy looks. He is just under six foot and built like a tank with tattoos on his forearms. His blond hair is cut short and neat and he always has a nice patch of light stubble on his jawline, especially in the morning. "Morning, handsome, you want breakfast in bed?" she giggles and sits beside him, removing his specs.

"What's this about Becky coming to stay?" he asks evenly.

Jane runs a finger along his face and under his chin. "Only for a few days, babe."

"You said as long as she wanted."

Jane sighs. "That's just a figure of speech. She's had a row with that half-head mate of yours. She just needs a time out."

Tommy pulls a face and pulls the covers over his head. Underneath the covers, he wonders what Gary might have done, apart from bearing his arse and dribbling. Knowing Gary, as he had done all his life, it could be a variety of all crazy things. He hears Jane padding out the room, he resurfaces and reaches for his glasses; he's blind as a bat without them. He puts them on and reaches for the phone.

Gary is sitting on the toilet, head in his hands when the phone rings...typical, he thought. Shuffling as fast as he could to reach it, Gary was hoping it might be Mrs Owegie asking for her batch of Walt Disney films, or Smelly Sid asking for his batch of porn films, or Becky saying she was sorry and was not really leaving him. Realistically, it was not going to be the latter as Becky had only left ten minutes ago. "Hello?"

"Gary, you tosser, what you done now?" Gary sighs and explains the series of unfortunate events leading up to Becky's departure. "Awww great! So now I'm lumbered with your bird round my gaff for God knows how long."

"Listen, once she's calmed down and Jane's made her see sense, she'll be back."

"If Jane makes her see sense, she ain't never coming back, you idiot. She'll probably be here for ever."

"What's that supposed to mean?"

"Jane knows what you're like mate, and Becky's her best friend."

"Ugh! Well your gonna have to talk to her and tell her I'm sorry and what a great guy I really am."

"So once again, I have to lie for you?"

"Yes. Now bugger off. I'm waiting for an important call and I'm half way through a pony." Tommy begins to protest but Gary hangs up. He begins to shuffle back to the loo when the phone rings again. "Bloody Tommy!" He picks up the phone, "I told you I'm taking a shi…"

"Hello, Mr Gary?"

The African accent, it was Mrs Owegie. "Oh, Mrs Owegie, hi. Sorry, how can I help?"

"Good morning, Mr Gary. I would like to know when I can come and get the videos? My sons are visiting from Nigeria for the week and the grandchildren will love to watch them?"

"Ah, yes of course. Well, give me half hour and I'll drop them off to you."

"Oh, that is wonderful, Mr Gary. I will see you in half hour. I will have the money waiting for you," she chuckles and bids him goodbye. Gary smiles and shuffles back to finish what he started.

An hour later and Becky sits in the lounge, with Jane comforting her. Tommy up and dressed, brings them both a cup of tea. Placing the drinks down, he asks them if they would like some breakfast.

"Thanks, but I'm fine," Becky replies, sniffing and dabbing her eyes with a tissue.

"You sure, love. I can do you a fry up if you like?"

Becky shakes her head and smiles. "You're a good bloke, Tommy, but honestly I'm fine. Wish Gary was more like you."

Tommy looks at Jane and smiles broadly.

"Oh, trust me, Tommy has his moments of stupidity." Jane says.

"No, I don't!"

Jane smiles. "Errr, the casino rooms. Your thirty-fourth birthday last week!"

Flashback. Tommy had won a load on the roulette. Unfortunately, he'd got so drunk, he'd lost it all on the Black Jack table. He'd staggered back to the roulette table and found the nervous bloke he was speaking to earlier, still sitting there. The nervous guy smiled and Tommy grabbed him in a headlock. To Tommy, he was showing male affection. To the nervous guy, he thought he was going to pass out and die. Jane helped to release his grip, and Tommy smiled, and told her, he loves her. Losing on the spin, Tommy declared that the table was fixed and there must be a secret wire hidden under the carpet. Before Jane could tell him he's drunk, talking twaddle and stop him, Tommy dropped to his knees and began searching the floor. With a loud shout he stated he found the secret wire and pulled it. Half the casino was instantly plunged into darkness, and Tommy was forcibly ejected from the premises. Outside he got bundled into a cab by Jane but not before he'd punched the head bouncer, and having a punch like a mule can kick, knocked the bouncer out cold. Tommy was now in serious bother with his other half!

"Oh. Yeah. Errr, I'll think I'll go do a bit of work, love. See you later, Becky. Hope things work out." He hastily leaves, gets outside and jumps in his black cab. Engine on, foot down, and is gone.

Apart from Becky leaving him, Gary's morning wasn't too bad. Just after Mrs Owegie called, and after he'd finished in the bathroom, Smelly Sid had phoned, and wanted his dirty movies.

Gary had dropped the Disney films and the porn films off and stopped off at the local café. Whilst having a massive fry up to help his heartache, his long-time friend, James Austin, who had moved away from the manor a few years back, walks in. Gold-rimmed specs, slicked back hair and the smart blue blazer, James was still the same as Gary remembered him three years back. With his short brown gelled hair, cheeky grin, Pringle jumper and faded jeans, complete with a Sovereign ring and sunglasses. James thought the same of Gary.

"Hello, sunshine," greets James. Gary stands up and they give each other a hug. James explains he's driven over from Essex to see his aunt who has not been very well. She was highly eccentric and had cut herself off from the family years ago, all apart from James who she referred to as her "Jimmy."

He is working as a Senior Manager in a recruitment office. He's single again and at a loose end. He has also devoted his spare time to a club he'd joined, investigating the supernatural.

Gary stabs the last bit of bacon on his plate, and laughs, "You've always been into that mumbo-jumbo stuff."

"Oi, there's nothing mumbo-jumbo about it, son, trust me. I've seen things that would make you think twice. I'm off to Peterborough Monday, huge convention. Lasts all week." He lifts up his mug of tea and takes a sip.

"Chris, Len and Ernie are off Monday too."

James removes his glasses and gives them a clean.

"How long you here for then?" Gary asks, shovelling beans in his mouth.

"Till Saturday, then I'm driving back to Essex, packing my stuff for Monday. Where them three lunatics going too?"

Mopping some sauce up with a slice of bread Gary looks up and shrugs. "Some place up in the West Country, place called Drarkland."

Chapter Four

The changes had come slowly. They had come through dreams which were more like memories, but memories belonging to others. Graphic, powerful, sexual, glimpses of a secret passed on from further down the years.

The night was beautiful, the wind soft and warm, and the smell from the forest was enchanting as was the moon. The urge to leave the house was great; to run into the night and hunt...blood, the need for blood was overwhelming. The taste of flesh, fresh meat to be ripped, to be torn...to be devoured.

Muscles tense, hard as steel and behind the neck there is a burning pain. Gums recede, teeth grow, and hands begin to stiffen, bending into claws. The beautiful night silently calls, every hypnotic sound of Mother Nature can be heard, and time slowly passes.

The night has become day and you are walking into your room. Fatigue takes your body and sleep overcomes you. Your hands are dirty, your feet are dirty, and there is a coppery taste in your mouth.

Sleep, dreams, memories... remembrance as you lay on your bed.

You suddenly sit upright, and remember... and may god forgive you, but you smile.

The Drarkland village postman, stares at the gory remains of the fox that has been torn to pieces and half eaten. He makes the sign of the cross and rushes away.

Chapter Five

Friday night, and the Wayward Man's Rest is buzzing. Perfume and aftershave blend with cigarette smoke, and the juke box belts out 'We close our eyes' by Go West. Tracy the barmaid throws her head back and laughs as skinhead Pete whispers something in her ear.

Gary chats to some peroxide bit in a ra-ra skirt, who's wearing one glove and pink lippy. Ernie pushes his way through the crowd with a round of drinks on a tray. At the table Ernie heads towards James; it's his last night, and he talks to Chris about the unknown. Tommy chuckles as he sees Chris is scared, and Len smiles as he's got the night off courtesy of Fatty Jock, and unbeknown to the others he had, earlier, pugged his camera behind the bar in readiness for a surprise group photo. James looks up and sees Ernie with the tray of drinks. Ernie never really liked James on the account he would refer to him as Oddbod (*remember from earlier*) and as he stood there James couldn't resist, adopting his best, remarkably good Kenneth Williams voice, "Aww, here he is… good Oddbod."

The others laugh and in temper Ernie shakes the tray and makes a strange humming noise of disapproval. "Oh, bloody hell you two, pack it in," growls Tommy as the drinks start to spill.

James laughs, and Ernie places the tray down, still grizzling. "You miserable sod, was only having a laugh with ya," James says. Ernie's oversized lips puff out, the way they always do when he has the hump, and he salutes James with his middle finger.

Gary comes over to the table and pulls a cigarette from his box of JPS; he has that smug grin on his face.

"You seem happier than you did earlier?" Chris enquires.

"Yeah, I'm well in with that tart over there." Glancing over, the girl in the ra-ra skirt smiles and waves. Len scowls. "Not that I'm gonna do anything mind, not while there's a chance with Becky."

"In that case, maybe the young lady would care for a drink with me." Chris begins waving.

The girl looks disturbed, there seemed to be a chubby bloke resembling a guinee pig waving at her.

"Not with that dopey shirt on, son." Gary tugs the daffodil yellow garment in question. "Where d'you get it from?"

"You!" snaps Chris angrily.

"Did you? Oh, in that case, it's a proper nice shirt. I got some red and blue ones in the van."

Chris mumbles something under his breath and reaches for his cocktail...*yes, cocktail, with all the trimmings.* "So, James, you were saying about strange goings on?" Chris continues with the conversation of the supernatural. Why, is anyone's guess, as he'd only end up sleeping with the light on.

James sips his lager and nods. "Strange goings on indeed, and on our own doorstep. Why, London alone is one of the most haunted places on earth and then you got the countryside... the Shropshire Skull for instance."

"What, er... what is the Shropshire Skull?" Chris asks nervously.

James takes a sip from his drink and leans forward.

"Let me tell you the extraordinary tale of the Shropshire Skull."

And so, the tale begins...

...It's 1976 and a group of friends from Dudley have decided to go caravanning in Shropshire.

They pull up late afternoon, parking themselves and the caravan in a small clearing right next to a forest and overlooking a sparkling crystal lake. They feel happy to be the only people around.

The group of four is made up of two men, Barry and Johnny, and their girlfriends, Sally and Vivian. They are all in their early twenties.

It's the summer of '76 and a right scorcher. Barry hands everyone a cold coke, whilst Sally pulls out the sun cover from the caravan door for them to sit in the shade.

They sit and exchange remarks over the beauty spot they have discovered. Vivian remarks on three days of relaxation and Johnny jokes about missing the motor racing.

Vivian playfully slaps him, and the group fall into laughter.

A while later after setting up the BBQ, Barry realises he needs some buns for the burgers. Sally reminds him about a store a few miles back, so he and Johnny drive off to get some... and some beers for later.

The two ladies stroll arm in arm to the lake. The water is so clear, and they remove their shoes and gently walk in until the water reaches just below their knees. Vivian shields her eyes and gazes up at the sky. Sally, however, unlinks her arm and bends forward to stare at something laying on the lake's bed.

Vivian looks towards her friend and enquires what it is she doing, Sally reaches in the water and returns with a strange-looking skull in her hands.

Vivian pulls a face as Sally turns towards her, displaying her find.

The skull looks like it could have been that of a huge dog and to be honest, it's not something Sally would dream of touching let alone pick up, but for some strange and unbeknown reason she finds it oddly fascinating.

Vivian feels the opposite and tells her to throw it back, but Sally ignores her and begins to leave the lake and walk back to the caravan with her grizzly find.

The men soon return with the buns, the beer and two bottles of Blue Nun wine. Sally retrieves the skull from inside the caravan and the men excitedly study it.

Barry thinks it's a dog's skull, but it must have obviously been a big beast due to the size of it.

Vivian sighs and tells them to get rid of it but they all chuckle and give her a glass of wine. A few glasses later and the skull is forgotten about.

So, they cook the burgers, drink the beers and wine and by ten they are feeling tired with all the country air, heat and booze!

Johnny opens his eyes. Was that a knock on the caravan door or did he dream it? He looks across to Vivian who, with him, sleeps on the put-up bed in the caravan's front room. Vivian's breathing is slow and even. He lays back down and as he closes his eyes the knock comes again... he wasn't dreaming.

Johnny sits bolt upright; his sudden movement doesn't wake his girlfriend but causes her to stir and cuddle towards him. Johnny, careful not to wake her, slowly edges away and gets to his feet. He wonders who is knocking this time of night? He walks towards the door but then suddenly stops as instinct warns him to be careful. He looks through the door's window, but nothing is there. He strides to the centre window of the caravan and peers out...nothing to be seen, only night. Maybe he did imagine it! After all the beers and wine he sunk earlier. Turning, he jumps as the figure stands behind him!

Barry apologises for making him jump, all that drink and he needs the bathroom. Johnny tells him about the knock on the door and explains he must be hearing things. His friend laughs then suddenly the knock comes again; this time both men hear it. Barry moves towards the door and is just about to open it when his friend grabs his wrist. He tells him not to open it; he has a very bad feeling.

They both move the small curtain and once again this time with Barry, peer through the window... nothing!

A sudden feeling of uneasiness passes between the two men, made suddenly worse by Vivian who screams and points towards the main window.

Sally comes rushing from the bedroom. Johnny is by Vivian's side, holding her. Barry looks through the window but like Johnny earlier, sees nothing.

Vivian was woken by the two men talking next to the front door. She lay in bed and glanced towards the window and that's when she saw the large shape!

Along from the living/bedroom just before the kitchen, is a small table. They now all sit there and discuss what has happened, Vivian, still shaken, describes what she saw.

"Just a large dark shape of man but then it twisted into the shape of a large dog or wolf."

There is silence among them and then, before anyone can speak, the knock on the door comes once again. There is a frozen silence and a racing of hearts.

The knock begins again and again and again, louder and louder it gets. Vivian clasps her hands over her ears as Johnny clasps his arm protectively around her shoulders. He looks to Barry who looks nervously back. Sally stands up and walks towards the kitchen where from the side she retrieves the skull.

The knocking turns to banging. The door handle, which is locked, turns violently up and down. Sally, holding the skull, moves towards the door almost trance like. Barry jumps up and moves towards her. Johnny looks on, eyes wide and terrified. He tightens his hold on Vivian.

Now the caravan begins to rock as some sudden force pushes against it. Vivian releases a scream and begins to sob. Johnny buries his head towards hers as Barry stumbles and falls to the floor. Getting to his feet he looks towards Sally; the caravan door is now open wide, and Sally has gone.

Barry shouts as waves of panic rush over him. He races towards the door, but it slams shut leaving him grasping at the handle...but the handle is stuck, as if someone or something has it held tightly. Barry, with all his strength, tries to turn it but it's unmovable. Releasing his grip, he looks through the window and catches the sudden movement of something large. Once again he tries the door handle; this time it opens, and Sally is standing there. She falls forward and Barry catches her.

They sit around the table. Johnny, who has a bottle of brandy in his suitcase, pours them all a generous measure.

They ask Sally what happened outside? She tells them that she was wrong in removing the skull from the lake and that she had returned it from where it had once come from. They ask her what was it out there? But she tells them there was nothing. They continue but she shakes her head and refuses to speak about it. Barry notices a fine single silver strand in her dark brown hair. They stay where they are, dozing in and out of sleep until the morning comes, then they pack up and leave... to this day, Sally will never talk about what was outside the caravan.

Chris feels a cold chill run down his spine. He grabs his cocktail. Draining it, he places the empty glass on the table. He thinks about the skull and the beast. He glances at Ernie.

"Ernest... have you ever been to Shropshire?"

"No! And don't call me Ernest!"

So, the evening goes on. Chris changes the conversation from the unexplained to the pending trip to Drarkland. Gary and Tommy began singing Chelsea songs much to the annoyance of skinhead Pete. Ernie eats twelve bags of pork scratchings and

James, after getting the ra-ra skirt's number in case he is down this way again, reminds Len that Gary's middle name was Ian.

"Yeah, I know," Len said, lifting his pint.

James grins. "Yeah, but put his initials together."

Len sits and concentrates; suddenly he bursts into laughter. "GIT!" he cries and points at Gary.

Gary looks over. "Listen Len, you mouthy sod, I'm doing my best to get your sister back. I've apologised for my actions but don't bloody give it or you'll cop one... got it?"

Len bursts into laughter once again. Gary looks confused. "No, I mean your initials, Gary Ian Taylor... GIT!" Everyone starts to chuckle.

"And he's right, you are a git... a right swindling git."

Gary spins round to see a middle-aged, thin, scruffy-looking bald bloke with a northern accent growling at him; it is smelly Sid.

"Bloody hell, what's this? Have a go at Gary night?"

"No," barked Sid. "It's, why has Sid got ten Disney films night?"

Mrs Owegie and her son, or should I say, sons...all three of them, sit in her living room. It was late when they arrived in England, so the two grandchildren had, after some supper, gone straight to bed. It was about twelve at night. When they had finished talking, she kissed them goodnight and made her way up to her room, happily knowing that for the weekend, and the rest of the week, she would have her sons back.

The three brothers sit and continue to talk, they are big men and the smallest, who was taller than Ernie and wider than

Tommy, was nicknamed "Tiny," and it was Tiny who spotted the films his mother had got for the grandchildren. "Oh, look at all the films mother has for the children, Walt Disney films. I remember these from our childhood."

The other two brothers come and look. "Dumbo, this was always my best, let's put it on."

Tiny smiles and agrees with his eldest brother, Mo. "Yes, this was a lovely film, I agree."

They chuckle like three big kids. Tiny bends forward and inserts it into the video recorder. Kim, the second oldest, grabs the remote and presses play. The three giants all sit there with big grins, a return to childhood.

Now, it might have said 'Dumbo' on the label…but this film definitely wasn't Dumbo, though there was some form of trunkage on display.

The smiles from their faces drop, as does the remote from Kim's hand, and just as things couldn't get any more shocking, their mother walks in the living room. "I forgot my water, I…" She stops in her tracks, glances at the TV and faints.

Earlier back in the pub.

"So, what you going to do lad?" Sid hisses.

Gary moves Sid away from his table and towards the corner of the pub. The pong of garlic, blended with B.O. assaults his nostrils; no wonder he's called smelly Sid. "Sid listen, first thing in the morning I'll go and see my marketing department and amend any problems for you mate. I guarantee the issue will be resolved and you, my friend, will have your artistic videos with you by lunch time."

"Artistic videos? I want my dirty films."

Gary frowns. "Same bloody thing, you silly old so and so."

"Oh, OK, but no later than lunch time… bloody frustrating sitting there all ready to go and flaming Dumbo comes on the box."

Gary feels his stomach turn. "Too much information, mate. Now bugger off and I'll see you tomorrow. You're ruining my evening, you old sod."

Sid curses under his breath and leaves the pub. Gary goes back to the others who are busy drinking… apart from Len, he is laughing and repeating the word 'Git'.

The night progresses. Len is chatting up Tracy and seems to be doing quite well. Ernie, now pissed, has put Iron Maiden on the juke box and is in the centre of the bar headbanging, much to everyone else's displeasure. James has disappeared and so has the girl in the skirt. Tommy is at the bar with Chris getting in some more drinks. Gary has gone to the van to get an electronic chess set to sell to Chris.

Skinhead Pete straddles up next to Len; three of his mates accompany him. Tracy has gone to change a barrel, and Len is stood there awaiting his moment when he could try out his camera. "That's mine son."

Len looks up and Pete glares down at him, his shaven head covered in scars, his neck muscles throbbing. "Hello Pete. Sorry mate, what's yours?" Len asks nervously.

Pete grabs Len by the front of his shirt and places his nose next to his. "The skirt," he replies threateningly.

"The skirt's yours, is it mate? What, you taken to dressing up in birds clothing?" Tommy chuckles and grabs Pete's hand, removing from it Len's shirt. "'Cause, I tell you something prat face, you touch my pal again and you'll be in a hospital gown."

Pete snatches his hand away. His three pals knew how dangerous Pete could be, but they also knew how hard Tommy was; there was a nervous exchange of looks between them. Gary approaches, holding the chess computer. He sees the confrontation. He hates skinhead Pete, and for years they'd goaded each other. "Look, boys," he addresses the group, "I really ain't got a problem with you three, but this bald-headed twat really gets my back up, so you either piss off and take him with you, or me, Tommy and Len are gonna take you outside and iron you out." He looks at Len, "Well, me and Tommy anyway."

The three thugs take a step back. Skinhead Pete threatens they haven't heard the last of this and eventually joins them as they disappear into the crowd. Len runs a hand through his spikey hair and puffs his chest out, "I was so close to landing him one," he squeaks.

Tracy returns to the bar and smiles. "You want it yet, Len?"

Bloody hell, thought Gary, he was doing alright with her.

"Yeah, go on let's do it."

A look of confusion passes between Gary and Tommy as Tracy hands the long, metallic object to Len. Chris, now that the unpleasantness is over, walks over to join them, "What's that contraption?" he asks, scratching his head.

"A Victorian Plate camera," Len proudly announces.

"But why?" Chris replies.

"To take pictures, why d'you think?" Len starts to set it up, placing it upright on its three-pronged legs. A few people stop what they're doing and gather round to look. "I've been spending time refurbishing it. It's become a hobby of mine and now it's done, I'm gonna take a picture of you lot of me mates."

"Does it work?" Tommy asks.

"Dunno! First time I've tried it is now."

Len gathers his friends into a group. Darting behind the camera, his head disappears under a dark flap. "After three, all say git," he announces.

"Haaa, oh Gary... git!"

"I thought it was supposed to be cheese?" Chris says.

Tommy shrugs, Ernie picks his nose and Len gives the countdown.

"GIT."

A unison of voices followed by an enormous white flash, a boom of thunder and then chaos.

There are screams form the women, Ernie and Chris to be included. Shouts of fear and panic from the men. Those near the entrance run outside and those who aren't take refuge under tables and behind chairs. Tracy the barmaid ducks behind and then jumps so quick her breasts flop out of her top. Gary, somehow in the mayhem, manages to spot this. The landlord runs into the optics shouting, "red alert," as to why no one knew. Safe to say, for a while in the pub it was pandemonium.

The smoke from Len's camera starts to clear. Tracy shoves her boobs back in her top and everyone slowly comes out from behind chairs and from under tables. Don continues to repeatedly say "Red Alert" to the optics but eventually things begin to settle.

"What the bloody hell was in that?" Gary cries as he pushes Len's head against the camera.

"DON'T!" Chris screams, grabbing Gary's arm.

"Why? He deserves a clump," Gary angrily protests, shrugging Chris's arm away.

"I'm not bothered about you hitting Len's head, just not on that contraption of doom," he points nervously at Len's camera. "It might set it off again."

"Oh, I see. I'll take him outside and batter him." Gary grabs Len by the scruff of the neck, but Tommy pulls him away.

"It wasn't my fault," squeals Len.

Chris pushes his hair from his eyes and grins sarcastically, "Leonard, you were the one who brought that… that weapon in here! You were the one who filled it with gunpowder…and you were the one who pulled the TRIGGER," Chris bellows out, the buckles on his sandals rattle in time with his nervousness and temper.

Chris was wearing buckled sandals with white socks. This really hasn't much bearing on this story, but it feeds character development. Anyway, small footnote. (See what I did there?)

Things calm down. Don eventually stops saying "Red Alert" and tells them he is going to call the police and worse, bar them all for life. Chris persuades him not to. Tommy threatens to hurt him, and eventually it was agreed no real harm was done.

Chris leaves to go home. Indoors and in bed he thinks about James' tales of the supernatural…he sleeps with the light on.

Gary sits at a table with Len, talking about Becky. Tommy puts a tune on the juke box, Relax! As Frankie Goes to Hollywood, Ernie goes to the kebab shop. The evening in the pub comes to an end and the patrons of the Rest stagger off home.

Later, Gary lays alone in his bed. He thinks of Becky and wonders if it might be an idea to drive round to Tommy's and speak to her in the morning.

Suddenly a thought pops into his head.

Smelly Sid! The videos he got...or rather didn't get, were from the latest batch Len put labels on. Gary sits bolt upright.

So, if Sid got Disneys then Mrs Owegie got... "OH, MY GOD!"

Saturday Morning, Gary's up and about early. He sits in his transit van across the road and a few doors down from Mrs Owegie's house. He hopes, he prays it's not too late. Before he can get out the van, her front door opens. Three men leave the house. One big, the second bigger and the third, massive. They wave their mother back in, one holds a piece of paper. "Is that the address?" one asks in a heavy African accent.

"Yes, now let's get going. I want to break some bones," the largest one shouts as they begin to get into a blue hire car.

Gary chooses to stay in the van and to heed the words of Wham's latest t-shirt craze, 'Choose Life'. They're here for a week, he remembers Mrs Owegie saying. He needs a plan. He needs to kill Len too, and see Becky, but right now the latter can wait. He turns on the engine and an idea turns in his head.

"Oh no. No, you're bloody not," Chris replies as he paces around his shop. "Oh no! You seem to forget I've been on holidays with you before."

"Yeah, and we had a laugh," Gary declares.

Chris rushes towards him, his face takes on a mask of pain as he remembers previous trips. "No, Gary, you had a laugh," he pokes Gary's chest, "but when you did, everyone else suffered and me more than most. I got beaten up. I got my head shaved, and last time on a trip with you, I had French police draw their guns on me."

Chris holds the top of his head with one hand, and fans his face with the other. He sits down and releases a very melodramatic sigh.

Ernie grins, his lips turn up giving the appearance of two saveloy's stuck to his face. "Remember when Gary got you to go to the gay bar and…"

"Shut up, idiot," hisses Gary, and kicks Ernie in the shin. He walks over to Chris, placing a hand on his shoulder and gazes down upon his crestfallen friend.

Chris looks up, tears seem to be forming in his eyes, he knows it's pointless to argue with him, but he tries, in fact he pleads. "Please don't come on my holiday. I've looked forward to this for ages."

But it's too late. Gary has made up his mind. "Chris, I promise you I'll behave. Me and Tommy… well, we're more mature now."

Chris sits bolt upright in the chair. "Tommy?"

"Yeah, he's coming too. I saw him earlier. Apparently, Jane and Becky are doing his swede in, so he needs a break."

Gary smiles and Chris once again releases another melodramatic sigh. He flops back into the chair. "It's started! I haven't even got there yet, and it's started."

Chris gets up and walks to the back of his shop…and swears loudly.

Once again, another customer walks in, and then out with a shocked expression on their face.

Monday

Gary, looks outside his window noticing the coast is clear. He leaves the flat and gets into his van and pulls away. Moments later, a blue car pulls up and three large Nigerian men get out.

Ernie's mother doesn't bother to call her son, she just simply begins to place six rashers of bacon in a pan and fries them. Ernie's eyes are closed but his other senses awaken. He rises, leaves the bedroom and descends the stairs, all the time eyes closed, and all the time in the same pants and vest.

Chris packs the chess computer he's purchased from Gary in his suitcase and closes it. He reaches for the shirt of choice...the red Hawaiian. Looking in the mirror he gels his hair back and pops a pimple. He puts on his sun glasses. He can hear the tune for Magnum PI playing in his head and wonders if he should grow a moustache. Reaching for his sandals and white socks he begins to consider the option of some face fur whilst on holiday. Buckled up and ready to rock, Chris points his finger at the mirror, makes a gun sound, blows his finger tip and smiles. He picks up his 'Friends of forests' book and leaves.

Tommy kisses Jane goodbye and grabs his Head sports bag. Becky is still sleeping off last night's emotional wine and 'why are men such bastards?' evening in the spare room. Tommy tells Jane that Gary is going away too, to give her some time to think and hopes to meet her for a talk and a meal when he returns. Jane tells Tommy that Gary is a complete arse...to which Tommy agrees. As he walks outside, Gary pulls up in the van. Jane scowls and slams the door. Tommy shrugs and Gary lights up a cigarette. The Lebanon by the Human League comes on, and they drive off.

Len, meanwhile, holds a picture of Len Jnr and smiles. He hopes he can take him on a small break during the summer holidays, even if it's just to Margate. Popping the photo inside his white Adidas track suit, a fake one Gary flogged him, he looks in the mirror and touches his bruised eye, a whack he got off Gary the other night due to the video-gate incident. He rubs his spikey hair, squirts on some Mandate aftershave. Looking at the clock he notices it's nearly eight and Chris will be there any minute. He gets his case, gets his wallet and in the corner, he gets his camera.

Chris turns up to collect Len. They argue about the camera, but Chris gives in when Len begins to scream. They drive to Ernie's who is standing outside his house dressed in leather and denim. His mum stands beside him, she tries to kiss him goodbye and looks tearful that her baby boy is going away. Ernie avoids the kiss and tells her he's a Hells Angel and stomps off, grizzling again.

They meet Gary and Tommy in the café. Gary insults Len's aftershave and tells him he's got some better stuff in the van. Tommy insults Ernie because he should be using aftershave and stinks of B.O. and everyone insults Chris's shirt.

They eat a full English, have a cup of Rosie and make their way to the motors. Ernie farts and Chris regrets that Ernie's travelling in his car.

Gary pulls away first. In Chris's car, Ernie moans he is still hungry. In Gary's van, the radio's on and Duran Duran, Hungry like the Wolf, blares out.

Chapter Six

Tobias Wilks sits in the Sheep's Head tavern and waits for the others to come. It's eight thirty on a Saturday morning, and though the tavern is not open for its thirsty patrons yet, it is open for business of another kind, of a secret and dark kind.

A ray of morning sunshine beams through the window and spotlights the wood on the table that Wilks sits at. He notices the tiny scratches imbedded into the oak. As his mind drifts from the pending troubling subject, a bang rattles the tavern's door. He jumps, and his mind snaps back to the present. He runs his fingers through his curly white hair. He stands up, walks towards the door and unbolts it.

"Morning, Tobias." He is greeted by a tall thickset man with thinning gingery-grey hair. His name is Johnathan Turner, and he owns the butchers. Behind him, David Dorie the postman who discovered the grizzly remains of the fox, and Harrold Green, the owner of the large farm near the top of the village, stands at the back.

"Come in." Wilks's voice is low and solemn. The men follow him to a family-sized wooden table and sit down.

"It's returned," Wilks' words hang in the air; there is an uneasy shift between them and something else… fear.

The night before and the stranger makes his way off the main drag and into the forest that boarders Melton, Winburt, South Wexted and Drarkland.

The forest was vast and for someone looking to hide out for while, it was ideal.

The man's name was Terrance Tyler. He was a large, brute of a man that should have been locked away in an asylum and never let free.

Tyler had been working as an enforcer for a gang boss back in London. Tyler's uses ranged from drug peddling, torture and even murder; the latter two he carried out with great satisfaction.

Tyler, though, had a twisted dark secret and it was this secret that had caused him to flee from the capital and head down to the West Country.

Tyler had holed himself up in a B&B in the heart of Melton Town. However, he had been found. The gang boss, Billy Chambers, a notorious villain, had sent three of his best boys down to deal with Tyler but his best boys however, weren't that successful. In fact, they were all dead, one with a broken bottle embedded so deep in his neck he was nearly decapitated, the other strangled with a sock of all things and the last punched repeatedly to death, his face completely obliterated to mush.

He fled the scene but so high on drugs and drink he crashed the car just outside Melton. Now he runs to the forest and the dark safety he hopes can hide him.

Tyler's brain is wired differently to that of a normal person. From the panic of escape it switches to joy, the joy remembering the destruction done to the heavies Chamber's sent.

He raises his massive bald head and howls into the night. Laughing, he runs ape-like deeper into the forest, the full moon giving him some light along his way.

Standing still, it hears the howling. Raising its muzzle towards the sky it senses something. It lowers itself to all fours and follows the scent.

A small creature darts off in the distance; tonight it has been given a pardon, there is a bigger, meatier prey at large. Moving at a speed faster than a race horse and agility equal to a cat, it runs through the night. Through the forest.

Tyler begins to breath heavily and stops for a rest, leaning against a tree, his clothes covered in blood and dirt. He starts to think of a plan. Even his child-like mind knows that the forest may hide him for one night but once the bodies are found in his room, it will be only a matter of time before the police find him.

His thoughts change and memories of his sick, perverse deeds seep into his head. He grins, teeth broken and rotten appear as his smile broadens and drool rolls from his lips.

It was Chamber's close friend's ten-year-old daughter that Tyler kidnapped, abused and finally killed.

She wasn't the first; there had been others before.

The sick bastard took polaroids, pictures to keep him company, to pleasure him and it was these pictures that

Chambers found when Tyler dropped his wallet in the office at the Silver Bay night club, a club owned by Chambers himself.

Tyler knew, when he got home and discovered his wallet was missing, that it wasn't going to be long before his wallet was found along with the pictures. Taking all his cash and a car, he fled.

Oh, how he wished he had that wallet now…the pictures!

He hears a snap of movement.

It slows down. Its muscles settle and standing up on hind legs, it sees the bald hulk that glares into the night, into its direction.

The man moves forward, he must be at least six-and-a-half feet tall. He wears a shirt, his muscles bulge underneath the material, his bull-like neck strains against the collar.

It steps out as the man steps forward. It senses no fear, only hatred.

Tyler can't believe his eyes. It's nearly midnight, he's in the middle of a forest and some joker is out here dressed as a, well, dressed as something very peculiar indeed.

"You've got to be a very strange person to dress like a freak and wander around the woods at such an hour," Tyler's voice was completely unsuited to his appearance. Instead of being deep and gruff, it was high pitched, almost sing song.

It stands still and watches.

"Aren't you going to say anything? I'm interested to learn how you're so tall…why your taller than me, or is that just part of your freak suit?"

Still, it does not move.

Tyler steps closer.

"I want you to take that costume off, freak, and I want you to do it now. I hate costumes and I hate you. I'm gonna hurt you, freak, but before I do I want you to take that stupid costume off. I want to see your face when I crush the life out of you. You see, freak, you've just met the bogeyman." Tyler breaks into laughter, he considers removing his trousers and shorts, his brain is firing in all directions, death, sex, hate...rage. He lumbers forwards surprisingly quick for a man of his size.

It moves.

Its fingers from one hand closes around Tyler's neck whilst the other shreds his stomach; entrails spill out like steaming worms, glistening and twisting in the light of the moon...it's that quick, that easy.

He can't breathe, let alone scream.

It lets go of his neck. Tyler drops to the ground...now it senses and smells the fear.

It drops to all fours and slowly stands over him. The eyes, he sees its eyes and he now knows what it truly is, a madman is turned sane... and then he is torn to pieces.

Wilks sits back and looks upon the others.

"The fox, the sheep, the signs, everything's pointing to you know what."

The others nod. Green gets up to stretch his legs. He paces around and decides to roll a cigarette.

He looks at the painting on the wall, the horse and cart leaving the forest with a certain haste, the night's sky lit up with a moon that's full and bright.

Nothing's painted apart from the aforementioned and trees, but he knows that it's there, in the woods, amongst the trees and shadows and he knows it's there in the forest of Drarkland and in the village. Someone has the curse, like an airborne parasite it drifts and lands and then takes control until either the victim dies of old age or is killed.

And then it leaves, leaves but never goes.

He looks once again at the painting.

"You and your horses will never make it home."

Wilks and the two other men look toward him.

"What?" asks Turner.

Ignoring his question, Green walks over.

"There's outsiders now, Beckett's Bed and Breakfast, the arrival of others will make things worse."

"I've spoken to him and he's agreed to keep the booking he's got until the end of next week and then he's taking no more until this is all over," Wilks tells them.

"If it's ever over," Dorie injects, looking fearful and tired.

They all sit and speak some more, they speak quietly, they speak of the curse, the legends, the horrific events befallen on the village throughout not just the years, but the centuries.

Eventually they take their leave. As they do, from the edge of the forest, only a stone's throw from the tavern, someone watches.

Chapter Seven

Later in the day.

While Gary and Chris drive through the town of South Wexted, Scarlet Malloy and Sara Hills pull into the car park of the Black Crow Bed and Breakfast, Drarkland.

Stepping out, they walk to the boot of the car to get their cases.

"That was some drive," huffs Sara, lifting her case then Scarlet's out of the boot.

"Sara, I'm going to buy you a double gin and tonic. Trust me, you are a star and, in this heat. No more driving today for you."

Sara chuckles. "I'm going to take you up on that."

They gaze towards the Black Crow; there is a stone footpath set in gravel that leads to the front entrance.

The building itself is quite impressive with natural stone cladding and even gargoyles, grotesques, looming from the roof. Creeping vines climb along and upwards and the many windows all gleam in the day's sunshine. Rows of various coloured flowers regimentally surround the base of the house and the steps that run up to the door.

As the birds sing, both women agree that Drarkalnd is just the perfect place to rest, relax and laze away the week. After having taken a boozy trip to Majorca a couple of months back, this would be an idle break to recharge their batteries.

Scarlet pushes her sunglasses up to rest in her long jet-black hair, her green eyes sparkle in the sun.

Her skin is tanned, and her white denim shorts and white t-shirt hug her slim figure and emphasise her colour.

She smiles with ruby red lips, displaying beautifully white teeth.

Sara pushes her sunglasses up to rest in a mound of curly ginger hair.

She squints and scratches her huge bottom with stubby, chubby fingers. Being ginger, her skin is already turning red and blotchy. She pulls a Mars bar from her purse and finishes it in two bites.

She wipes her chocolate-covered hand on her floral pattern dress, well, not all floral as there's a picture of a large parrot on the back and picking up her case once again, heads to the building.

As the two women walk into the reception area, Norman Beckett walks down the stairs and greets them with a broad West Country accent and an even broader grin.

They return the salutations.

"You've travelled all the way from Beckenham, Kent, aye? Some journey that is. In fact, I've got a party of gentlemen not far from your neck of the woods due to arrive today as well."

Sara looks at her friend.

"Ewww, maybe their hunky and funky," she laughs and smiles. Beckett notices she has chocolate stains on her front teeth.

Beckett explains a bit about the Black Crow and the village. He tells them that there is, thirty miles west of Melton, a nice beach and coastal spot.

The women are given a key and shown their room.

"Feel free to relax in the lounge, play pool in the games room or sunbathe in the back garden. Anything you need just ring the bell on reception and I'll be at your service."

Beckett leaves them to unpack.

"Aww, weren't he a sweet old boy," Scarlett comments.

"Yeah, he's only tiny and he looks cute in his little red dungarees," adds Sara.

They laugh and begin to unpack their cases. The room is very pleasant. The carpets are light grey, and the walls are painted magnolia. The two single beds are made with fresh white sheets and a silver coloured quilt finishes them off. Pushing the grey curtains aside, the view shows the Black Crow car park and the beginning of the forest. There is a large oak cupboard and drawers for their clothes. Next to the wardrobe is a door that leads into the en-suite bathroom. Inside the bathroom there is a shower, karzie and a table with loads of towels.

Sara flops onto a bed and kicks her shoes off. Stretching, she looks towards Scarlett and smiles.

"Different to our Spanish adventure," she giggles.

Scarlett, who is gazing at the view, turns and grins.

"It's definitely going to be quieter, that's for sure," she replies.

Scarlett's mind wanders back to Majorca. It was a fantastic holiday, crazy and hazy, but fantastic. Pity all the men she met were sleaze-balls and only after one thing! Pity about Sara. The one thing she was after and she never got. Still you never know, maybe there's a handsome prince amongst the group of men due to arrive...you never know, there might be two. She sits on her bed.

"Might have a quick go at catching some rays in the garden. Shall we explore?"

Sara props herself up and nods.

"Be rude not to. I'll slip my bikini on and slip the bottle of gin from my case."

Laughing together, they begin to get changed.

Beckett walks to the kitchen. His friend, Ron Ayelsworth, sits supping at his bottle of cider.

"New guests?," he enquires. Ayelsworth is Beckett's closest friend and lives close by in a detached cottage, retired and in his mid-sixties. He loafs in his friend kitchen drinking and idly chatting.

"Yep, couple of girls from Kent."

"Young or old?"

"In their late twenties, I'd say."

"Oh! Would you give 'em one?"

"Would the dark haired one...dunno about the fat one, though."

Beckett sits down and lifts a pint glass filled with white wine.

The liquid just touches his lips when the bell in reception rings furiously and someone shouts out "OI."

"Bloody Londoners have arrived," he moans and makes his way to reception.

Gary and Tommy chuck their cases in the corner of the room and decide it's time to hit the pub.

"Stone me, that old git looked like a garden gnome in them daft trousers," Gary comments.

"Think you pissed him off calling him shorty and breaking his bell," Tommy replies.

"No, mate, I think that was because Ernie dropped one and stunk his reception out."

"Ugh, that bloke's not well, son. No wonder Chris looked ill, having to put up with his arse all the way here."

Chris lays on his bed and smiles. He has opened the window and is preaching to Len the benefits of fresh country air and how it would aid them into a peaceful and relaxing sleep.

Len was just glad to be away from Ernie's flatulence.

"It's the proper sticks out here," Len comments as he puts his swede out the window and gazes out towards the forest.

Chris agrees. "It is indeed, Len. No grey streets and vehicle fumes for us here oh no! Greenery and clean air for us." He begins to cough as Len accidently zaps him with deodorant spray.

Ernie sits alone on his bed. He opens his case and produces a large half-empty jar of pickled onions and a block of cheese. He opens the jar and places a large onion inside his mouth. Then he unwraps and bites a huge chunk out of the block of extra mature cheddar, washing this down with the juice from the pickled onions. He belches, stands up and ventures into the bathroom. He drops his trousers and pants and commences to insult the porcelain.

The bedrooms for guests are situated along the top corridor. From here there is the staircase that leads down to the Black Crow's lower level. The stairs are dark brown and varnished with a deep burgundy runner that blends with the deep burgundy carpet on the upper level and the large deep burgundy rug in the hallway and reception area. From here there are two doors, one that leads to the kitchen where the guests' food is cooked and the other leads into the lounge. The lounge is very spacious with a high ceiling and brown leather sofas and chairs. The walls are white with a huge bookcase housing hundreds of various books. The carpet is thick…and yep, you guessed it, burgundy! In the corner sits a TV and a nest of tables. A small pool table and dart board reside in an L-shaped corner. Continuing, you enter the dining room. The dining room is painted lemon and the double doors open out onto the patio. The fine thin white curtains gently move in the breeze and the sun shines onto the pine laminate flooring. There are tables and chairs dotted about and the tables are all dressed.

Soon the lounge is inhabited by Gary and co, minus Chris who's getting changed. Tommy is amazed by all the books on the shelves and wanders along, browsing the titles.

"It's like a bleedin' library."

Len laughs. "Oh yeah, and since when did you ever go in a library?"

"Oi you, ya mouthy sod, I like to read," Tommy growls as he threatens to throw a book at Len's head.

Gary looks at his watch and frowns.

"Bloody Chris. What's he doing up there? I reckon we should go and he can meet us in the pub."

Len and Ernie agree, Tommy shouts up the stairs.

"CHRIS! WE CAN'T BE ARSED TO WAIT ANYMORE MEET YOU DOWN THE BOOZER."

Beckett, who is used to gentler and quieter guests, jumps and looks painfully at his friend.

"Bloody Londoners."

Sara looks across to her friend. They are relaxing in the garden, catching a few rays of sunshine, unaware of the motley mob not far behind them, when she hears the shouting.

"Sounds like the boys from London have arrived," she chuckles and sips her drink.

"Shall we have a peek?" Scarlett sits up and places her feet in her flip flops.

Sara nods vigorously and they leave the garden, creeping quietly into the house.

They make their way into the dining room and through to the lounge, but the lads have just left. Sara pokes her head round into the hallway and spots him.

He is in his early to mid-thirties and of average height but carrying a few pounds. His dark hair is swept back to reveal a face full of character and there is a worldly knowledge in his eyes.

His attire is amazing and with each step his buckles rattle like a cowboy's spurs.

As he descends to the bottom of the stairs, Sara holds her breath. He catches her gaze; he smiles.

Scarlett looks as the tubby bloke in the loud shirt ambles down the stairs. He reaches the bottom, looks towards her and nervously grins. He wears sandals with socks and bears resemblance to a hamster or guinee pig.

He stutters a welcome and introduces himself as Chris Murren.

Sara releases a sigh and rushes forward.

"I'm Sara and this is my best friend, Scarlett."

"Nice to make your acquaintance." He wipes a clammy hand on his shorts and shakes hands with both women.

"Are there any more of you?" Scarlett enquires.

"Err, yes, there is. There's four more but they've already gone on the pi... gone to the pub!"

"Oh, yes, the Sheep's Head Tavern. We noticed that driving in," Sara remarks.

"I'm off to meet them now. Would, err, would you ladies care to join us?"

"That would be nice, Chris," Sara's response is quick and Scarlett smiles as Chris seems to become even more nervous.

"We'll meet you down there. We'll have a quick freshen up first," Scarlett tells him as she makes her way to the stairs.

Sara follows and stops to smile closely at him.

Chris smiles back, makes a funny breathing noise, then departs.

Gary pushes the door and the four men from London strut inside the tavern.

There is no juke box playing, no brightly-lit bar lights glowing and no sort behind the jump with massive tits to greet them.

Eyes fall upon them, even a collie dog stares as they look around and stroll to the bar.

The floor they tread on is wooden as are all the tables and chairs.

Lamps and candles are still in use, though not yet lit and there is a stuffy smell of wood, wax and beer.

Further along they notice a pool table which seems surprisingly out of place. There is a large painting on the wall; it depicts a scene where a man seems to be driving his horses and cart hard to get home, they are leaving a forest in which a large full moon sits in the sky.

The others pay it no attention, but Len feels a cold chill in his veins. For some reason, it unnerves him.

Behind the bar, an overweight man with thinning curly white hair stands and polishes a tankard.

He eyes them with suspicion and nods.

"Evening," he flatly greets.

Gary smiles and leans on the bar. He returns with a "Hi," and studies the pumps. There seems to be a wide range of bitter but very few lagers; he spots one agreeable to all and orders four pints.

"Pork scratchings!"

Wilks looks up… the beast! Then he realises it's just an odd-looking bloke who's with the others.

His nerves settle, and he begins to pour the drinks.

"We don't sell Pork scratchings," he replies to the creature.

Ernie frowns and flaps his arms.

"We sell crisps, and there's a bar menu if you want something proper to eat. The kitchen closes at nine and we don't take checks or cards, cash only."

Ernie grabs a menu and begins to study it.

"I'll have steak, chips and tomatoes, please, mate… do you get lots of chips?"

"The Mrs serves a generous portion," replies Wilks, sighing.

"Gary, don't. That's what the birds say anyway," scoffs Ernie.

Wilks shakes his head while Gary belts Ernie's.

"Errr!" Gary's hand feels greasy, he wipes it on the back of an unsuspecting Tommy's Sergio Tacchini track suit top and pays for the drinks.

He hears a sudden rattling and without turning around, indicates to Wilks to pour another pint.

Chris explains that he's met two ladies at the Black Crow and that they're joining them all for drinks.

"What you mean, you spoke to women?" Len asks.

Chris feels pained by the fact that Len was serious.

"Yes, Lennard and what's so strange about THAT?"

People start to stare, Gary laughs at the irony. Chris was the one looking forward to a calm week away and it was him that was causing all the raucousness.

"Calm down, for Christ's sake," laughs Gary, handing him a drink.

"These birds, what they like?" asks Tommy.

Chris describes them as they prop against the bar and sup their beer.

Time passes. Ernie collects his food and wanders off to sit down, receiving cautious and fearful looks from the locals.

Len and Tommy play pool. Len is wining, and Tommy can't understand how jammy he is.

The door opens. Scarlett and Sara walk in. Gary's jaw drops and from somewhere in the distance there's a fart.

She is a vision.

A vision as she steps into the tavern.

Her hair is long and dark, her skin tanned almost glowing.

Her body, slim but with curves that count and her face…

…Lips full and red, cheekbones high, above eyes that sparkle emerald.

Long tanned legs carry her towards him.

Next to her waddles a gingery fat bird.

"Gentleman, let me introduce you to Scarlett and Sara," Chris welcomes the two women to sit at the bar. The lads gather round to say hello… apart from Ernie, he stays sitting and eating his supper.

Sara sips her G & T, Scarlett settles for a white wine spritzer, they all fall into conversation.

Sara tells them that herself and Scarlett have known each other since secondary school and that they both work together at Alders department store in Bromley.

Gary, Tommy and Len are mesmerised by Scarlett and her bare legs, Ernie strolls over and nearly falls over his tongue.

"This is Ernest," Chris introduces the ape-like Hells Angel.

Nervously they smile and shake hands with him. Ernie leans towards Tommy and mummers, "I'd give the dark bird one."

81

"No chance," replies Tommy through the corner of his mouth.

"Anyone for pool?" asks Len. Before anyone can answer, Scarlett jumps up.

"Best out of three?"

Len looks up into her eyes and just mumbles… Three!

The others follow to the pool table, apart from Gary who can't buy cigarettes and leaves to buy some in the village shop before it closes… and Chris, Sara grabs his hand and virtually forces him to sit on Scarlett's vacated stool at the bar.

"So, Chris Murren, tell me all about yourself."

Gary walks into the village, finds the shop and steps inside. Walking to the counter, his mind forgets about the fags and rests on the vision in front of him… she is a vision, here we go again.

Her hair is long, wavy and brown with flecks of blonde and flicked at the front. Her eyes, mesmerising, hypnotic, they enthral him; so many colours, blue, brown, green, all swirling together.

Her body, her body is… I can't be writing any more of this descriptive, romantic stuff! Let's just say she's fit and any sane man would. Gary's smitten because he aint had a bit in ages and even if he had, you'd still want a bit from this sort.

Twice she must ask the daft sod what he wants. Eventually, he snaps back to normal and answers her.

She hands him the cigarettes and he hands her the money; a spark of electricity passes between them as hands touch. Don't worry, I'm not going all Mills and Boon; earlier the shop was carpeted with a nasty nylon thread that's got more static than the national grid.

She explains and apologises.

"That's all right, darling. It might have been a bit of chemistry, know what I mean?" He winks and grins, the sort behind the counter smiles and plays with her hair; always a good sign, that.

"Might have been," she giggles and sits back on her chair. "So, you down here for long?"

"For the week. We got here today and leave next Monday."

"I see, so I might see more of you then?" A smile plays along her lips.

"Oh, I guarantee you will, babe. You own this shop, do ya?"

"No, my brother does, him and my dad. I just help out. They live above it."

"And you?"

"I live a moment's walk in the woods. I've got a nice log cabin there." She leans across the counter, Gary leans towards her... those eyes.

"Oh, yeah, you live alone?"

"Sometimes," she answers in a low sultry voice.

"Dad wants you upstairs, Deloris." The voice cuts into the moment. Standing further behind her in the doorway is her brother, his face hidden by the shadows.

"OK, Tim. I'll lock up and come now." Her mood changes, Gary walks towards the entrance.

"I'll be seeing you then, Deloris."

A smile returns to her face as he leaves the shop.

"Maybe, Gary."

She knows his name.

He enquires how and her eyes flash.

"I'm the village witch, my dear," she laughs. He leaves. Moments earlier, Beckett was in the shop moaning about them, especially the mouthy one named Gary who broke his bell.

He hears the door close and lock behind him. The daylight is starting to fade; they say darkness comes quick in the country.

Someone watches him. Gary, unaware, continues towards the tavern.

Inside, the tavern is filling up. There is a jukebox after all and the Wurzels are playing. I'm not being stereotypical, but they are.

Len is still playing pool with Scarlett who's beating him. Tommy and Ernie stare as she bends over to pot a ball. At the bar, Chris sits with Sara.

So, the night goes on; they all get to know each other. It seems Sara is quite keen on Chris and as for Scarlett, she seems to be giving Len more attention than the others.

Tommy and Ernie hit the shots and strike up a conversation with some locals.

Gary thinks of Deloris. Those eyes were undoubtedly stunning but there was something else; it was like they held a secret.

He gave up and wondered how Becky was, then he thought about Deloris and the sizable boobs on her. Maybe he would visit that cabin in the woods...but not tonight, tonight was for drinking.

"Another round of shots, barman...for everyone."

He slams his money down, his friends cheer, some drunken locals cheer and pat him on the back, Ernie puts some coins in the juke box.

They get on one in the tavern while outside someone or something races into the forest; darkness has come to Drarkland.

The sensation when the change takes hold starts with a feeling of burning.

A sudden tingling of heat that builds up and up as if the blood itself is boiling.

At first, when the curse or gift, depending which way you look at it, takes place it becomes hard to control. As it occurs more often and with experience, it can be brought on at any moment, day or night. It does not need a full moon, though the moon, when full, raises the blood levels like the tides of the rivers and seas, making the beast even stronger.

After the burning, there is a rush of electricity to the brain. The limbs stretch, and the internal organs change, bones break and repair, teeth grow as do claws and hair.

Part of the brain remembers and melts into the beast's instinct, making it careful, when needed, to cover its tracks and kills.

As explained earlier in the story, memories from the beast are passed down along the bloodline of the curse; these occur mostly when the human form is resting.

The body of the beast is strong and huge; once transformation has completed it can reach a height of over seven feet, with muscles like steel it can destroy any living animal.

The beast is half way through a change now; it lays in the forest on its back, body morphing.

Patches of dark hair sprout, hatred and hunger begin to take over.

Flesh, blood, pain.

Muscles tense, stretch.

The change has virtually taken over now.

It releases a howl.

The howl isn't that of a typical wolf, but more of a guttural scream.

Inside the tavern, Wilks is glad that the juke box is fully turned up. Ernie's head banging to AC/DC. He and his companions only hear the thrash of guitars, but Wilks hears it as do the villagers; tonight is the night of the beast.

Tuesday

Sitting at the dining table, Sara and Scarlett thank Beckett as he brings them both a cup of tea.

"Breakfast won't be long, my dears. Kate has just put some bacon on to go with your sausages and eggs."

They thank him, and he leaves.

It's nine am and the day's warming up, and because it's such a beautiful warm sunny day, let me give you a descriptive geographical tour of Drakland village.

A DESCRIPTIVE GEOGRAPHICAL TOUR OF DRARKLAND VILLAGE

The road that leads into Drarkland village slopes downwards, in other words it's a hill (ref. beginning when Haines comes running down it). It is surrounded on both sides by the vast forest.

On entering the village, to your right is the general store run by Deloris's brother and father. To the left, keep driving or walking and your find the Black Crow Bed and Breakfast and the detached home of Aylesworth, which sort of bends round as his garden backs into the forest not too far from the river and about a five-minute walk from Deloris's log cabin.

Travelling back in the other direction, eventually you'll arrive in what is called the village square where you have the General Store, as previously mentioned on the corner, and various other small shops next to it.

Further up and facing into the square you have rows and rows of small houses, with more rows situated behind them. These are the people who live in Drarkland and their homes continue until they reach the forest that comes in from the westerly direction.

In the centre of the square there is a small fountain that is surrounded by a round stone wall. The village phone box resides next to it. From here, looking opposite from the General Store next to the end of the houses, is the Sheep's Head Tavern.

I hope you're keeping up with all this! it ain't easy to describe things you know... I've had to draw a map and everything.

...To continue. Next to the right side of the tavern are a few more houses and alleyway, and a few more houses that end where a massive hedge, part of the hedge that separates the Black Crow, begins.

If you go down the alley, there is the local Police Station (more about that later) and further on, a small church which also doubles up as a school for the village children. Sort of like the *one on "Little House on the Prairie" did. Younger readers, go Google the show. Older ones, if you remember this show with as much fondness as me, then you're a star! Great program with great characters and my favourite episode was the one where they played baseball and the... sorry, completely digressing!*

There is no hospital, but they do have a village doctor and midwife, think she's a midwife! Big, fat old bird with a turgid type look! They also have a dentist that is also the village vet.

Anyway, that's about it! If you've read this and thought, "Where's Deloris's mum?" Well, her mum died a few years back when she fell asleep drunk on the wall that surrounds the fountain and fell in the water and continued to sleep... in fact, she slept so much she drowned! To be honest, she wasn't sorely missed even by her family. She was a miserable old drunk who would get Oliver Twist (pissed) and wander around the village offending people and generally being a right git!

OK, so we've come to the end of the geographical tour, hope you enjoyed it and we'll go back to the Black Crow and the breakfast table where Scarlett and Sara sit and await their bacon, sausages and eggs cooked by Kate's fair hand. When I say fair hand, it is the only fair hand she's got as she had the other one lobbed off helping her cousin fix his mangle. Still, the mangle's working again and so is Kate, helping Beckett out in the bed and breakfast with the cooking, cleaning and general stuff. She doesn't really need to work but it's nice to keep your hand in... even if it is only the one!

Returning

Scarlett looks at the lily in the vase and smiles.

"Beautiful, simply beautiful." She sips her tea, though her head is slightly tender she intends to make full use of the day.

Ernie lies on top off his bed, on his back, his hands folded upon his chest like a corpse waiting for a coffin... then the smell drifts into his room and his nostrils. With closed eyes but heightened homing senses, he rises.

He strides towards the door and pulls it wide open. Eyes closed, he masterfully navigates his way to the top of the stairs.

Scarlett, still smiling, looks towards the dining room entrance and suddenly her smile is replaced by a mask of horror.

It stands there, its arms stretched before it. The face hideous and framed by long, dark greasy hair... with a blunt fringe.

Below, the body is mummified partly in a white vest and pants and covered in stains... oh, the stains, hellish!

It moves towards her. It's so close she notices the black gunk stuck between its hairy toes.

A sliver of spit rolls from the corner of its mouth as does a strange zombie-type noise.

"Ernie!" she recognises it/him.

Her outburst causes Sara to turn and she's confronted with the nightmare image before her.

She releases a scream and Ernie's eyes open wide.

Ernie begins to scream too. He is not indoors, and Sara is not his mum!

Sara, realising the ghoulish creature is Ernie, stops and puts her hand over her mouth. Ernie releases a guff of wind and Scarlett puts her hand over her nose.

Ernie stops his high-pitched scream and begins to grizzle, a bit like a wounded bear. Feeling exposed and vulnerable, he turns and flees embarrasingly away.

Chris leaves his room and heads towards the stairs. He's sure he hears screaming and starts his decent with a concerned look on his face.

His head is fragile from last night's session in the tavern and the dream he had last night has left him feeling uneasy.

Chris had a strange dream of wolves and demons and being chased in a wood. He pictures once again the monster's face when suddenly nightmares become reality.

Chris lets rip with an almighty scream of dread as the monster runs towards him.

The monster or Ernie screams back.

Len jumps up, falls out of the bed and screams in pain whilst Tommy screams to "SHUT THE FUDGE UP!"

Gary pulls the covers over his head and curses.

"WHY?" Chris shouts. Ernie doesn't answer, he just returns to his weird grizzling and rushes to his room, nearly knocking Chris down the stairs in his haste.

Beckett appears at the bottom of the stairs as do Scarlett and Sara.

Chris nervously fiddles with his lips and smiles. "Thought it was a monster."

Gary, Tommy and Len enter the dining room later, dressed casually in Lacoste polo shirts and England football shorts.

"Morning all," Gary says, smiling. He and the others join Chris, Sara and Scarlett at the table.

"Blimey, didn't expect to see you lot up so early," exclaims Chris as he shovels his beans.

"Neither did I, son, but after all that bloody screaming and hollering what do you expect," moans Gary.

"What the hell happened?" Tommy asks, puzzled.

Scarlett explains, not leaving out the bit about Chris screaming too.

It started with a chuckle which shifted to giggle a giggle becomes a laugh and then a laugh and a roar.

Gary, Tommy and Len, hurting with laughter and pointing at Chris.

Ernie appears once again in the doorway, this time dressed in clod-hopper boots, ripped jeans, a Motorhead t-shirt and a black biker jacket.

"Look, it's the other article," cries Len, pointing now at him.

There's a unison of mirth, apart from Chris whose face has gone beetroot. Ernie stomps in and sits down looking miserable.

Beckett arrives at the table; he informs Ernie to wear suitable attire when wandering around the house and not grubby pants and vest. He also tells him not to make so much noise.

Ernie tells him to bugger off and Gary calms the situation down. They order their breakfast and decide what to do with the day.

Sara shows Chris the road map. She taps the place named Hurlsworth Bay.

"Apparently, it's a very nice place with a beautiful sandy beach."

"Yes, sounds fantastic," he replies. "I'll go and see the lads and see who's up for it."

Sara looks as Chris walks off… ohhh!

Tommy, Len and Ernie are all in. They go to get their costumes and towels. Gary has popped to the shops. When asked why, he tells Len to mind his own business.

He comes back shortly, complaining about some bloke called Tim and a waste of a walk. He tells them he'll come and they all jump in Chris's car, apart from Scarlett who travels with Sara.

Chapter Eight

If you've ever been to St Ives in Cornwall, then Hurlsworth Bay is pretty much its twin.

If you haven't, please go Google it because I really can't be bothered to describe it.

The cars pull into an already full car park, the midday sun beats down and Gary could murder a cold beer.

Sara leads the way to the beach; they follow, hire some deckchairs and ogle Scarlett as she strips down to her bikini.

She asks Len to rub sun lotion on her back; Len nearly faints as does Chris when Sara asks him to do the same for her.

Ernie excitedly rushes into the sea. He's wearing speedos and has knocked a child over. He doesn't stop, he just keeps running till he can't run no more and falls into the surf.

Tommy and Gary go to the pub.

Deloris stands in her cabin and gazes into the forest. She drifted off last night into a dreamless sleep, a deep sleep, and for some reason her body aches.

She walks to her fridge. Opening it, she studies its contents and decides she's not that hungry.

She remembers her encounter with the handsome man from London, Gary, and smiles.

She turns on the radio and flops onto the sofa. Werewolves of London is playing. She lets her head fall back and begins to laugh.

"I mean this was a proper sort, the face the body," Gary is describing Deloris to Tommy as they sit outside the pub drinking cold beers from tall glasses. He has some bread from a roll he ate and is soaking the crust in some of his lager.

Tommy runs a finger along the glass and wipes the water away; the day is a scorcher.

"So, you gonna jump it or what?"

Gary sits back in his chair. He pulls the collar of his polo shirt up to cover his neck from the sun.

"I dunno mate, still got to sort things out with Becky. It doesn't help having her brother here."

"So, if Len weren't here to grass you up, you'd hump it?" Tommy laughs and raises his larger.

The cold amber liquid spills down his throat, giving instant satisfaction to his thirst.

"Yeah, I mean no... I mean, oh, I don't know what I mean or what to do."

Tommy drains the glass, belches and slams it down on the table.

"Why are you soaking that bread in your drink?"

Gary hurls the piece of bread in the air; a large gull collects it instantly in its beak.

"To rid the world of them buggers. South African geezer told me if you soak bread in booze and give it to seagulls, after a while they get drunk and flop out the sky."

"You rotten sod!"

"Nothing rotten about it, son. I'm doing everyone a favour... bloody flying rats."

Ernie strides from the sea like the creature from the black lagoon.

Kicking over a sandcastle that has taken some poor child ages to build, he drops into his deckchair and lets his arms flop over the sides. The chair creaks under his weight.

"Where's Tommy and Gary?" he loudly asks.

"The pub," Len replies.

"I'm starving; what's for lunch?"

"Dunno, aint given it much thought."

Ernie sits up and glares at Len like he's mad.

"But it's lunch time."

Chris leans over and chuckles.

"Then go eat. Were not hungry, Ernest."

"Don't call me Ernest," snaps Ernest.

Chris shakes his head and opens his sports bag. He removes a box with a picture of a chess set on it.

"What's that?" Ernie shouts.

Chris's face develops a pained expression.

"It's a chess computer, Ernie, and stop shouting you'll, wake the ladies."

Ernie gazes at the girls. Scarlett has her eyes shut and Sara is snoring.

"Why?" he announces.

Chris looks at him.

"Why what?"

"The chess computer, why?"

Chris looks from the computer to Ernie.

"Because I want to play chess, that's why."

Chris sets the chess computer up. Inserting the batteries, he begins to play.

Ernie wanders off to get fish and chips. Len looks at Scarlett then towards the sea… just maybe.

Tommy and Gary stare in amusement as Ernie walks past, unaware they are there. Wearing only his maroon speedos and clod-hoppers, he holds a large white paper parcel from which he lifts a large piece of battered fish and devours it whilst on the move. Pieces fall from his mouth as he smacks his lips together and barges between two men. They swear at him and he throws a piece of fish at their heads.

"He's like the missing bloody link."

Gary looks at Tommy and laughs.

"Yeah, he is. Mind you, I'm feeling a bit Hank Marvin now."

They finish their drinks, leave the bar and head for the fish and chip shop to partake in battered cod, chips and mushy peas.

"IT CHEATS!"

Len turns to see what Chris is shouting about, Scarlett opens her eyes and Sara stops snoring.

"Pardon?" Len begins to chuckle.

"The bloody chess computer I bought from Gary, it blooming CHEATS."

People nearby look towards the commotion.

"But how?" Len asks, still laughing.

Chris stares at the board and looks wildly at Len.

"What do you mean, how? It just cheats, it refuses to obey the rules and cheats. Typical, I should have known, bloody Gary Taylor and his cheating chess set."

Len lowers himself into the chair, hiding his amusement from Chris's glare, Scarlett turns away from Chris and faces him, she bites her bottom lip and tries not to giggle.

"Yes, I can see what you're both doing, and I can assure you both it's not funny." He throws the chess set on the sand and folds his arms. Glaring at it, he begins to sulk.

"What's wrong?" asks Sara opening her eyes.

Gary and Tommy arrive with their food; the smell of vinegar wafts into the air.

"What's up with him?" asks Tommy as he launches a chip at Chris's head.

"Ask bloody him," he indicates towards Gary.

Gary looks at Tommy and shrugs.

"What I done now?"

"It CHEATS! The chess computer you sold me cheats."

"Well, cheat back," Gary replies.

Chris picks up a piece and fires it in Gary's direction, missing him by inches.

"That's your answer, is it? Cheat back. You take an ancient Indian game of strategy, intelligence and skill and you just change it to fit the rules of a new form of chess invented by Gary Taylor. Well, NO, I won't cheat back but I will have my money back."

"Alright, we'll sort it out later, you touchy git."

Tommy bursts into laughter, he points at Chris and sits down into his deckchair, the chair collapses and his fish and chips spill into his lap along with the mushy peas. He sits bent in two, disbelieving in what has happened.

"Check mate, Thomas," Chris announces. Putting on his sunglasses he lays back in his chair and smiles. "Check mate."

Ernie eats his lunch as he continues to walk along the pier.

He stops to look at the arcades and notices a rather nice toffee apple stall. Wandering to have a closer look, his eye catches a small hut next to it, a hut with the words, Madam Kazel, painted in swishy gold letters.

He walks towards it; the door is open, shielded only by beaded curtains.

Laura Kartman or as she's known in the psychic world, Madam Kazel, sits and rests her eyes.

She is a reader of tarot cards, tea leaves and palms. She has conducted séances, participated in Ouija boards and organised ghost tours. Today she sits in her hut and readies herself with the all-seeing knowledge of the mystic ball.

Laura, since a child, has always had the gift to see things others cannot, to reach beyond the veil and communicate with the departed… and since losing her job at the bingo hall, becoming a medium wasn't a bad option.

She releases a gasp as the head suddenly appears through the curtains. For a minute she thinks an Incubus has descended from the otherworld but on closer inspection she realises it is the head of an extremely strange looking man.

"Who seeks the wisdom of Madam Kazel?" she goes straight into character.

The man steps inside.

"Errr, me."

She notices, which to be fair ain't hard, that the tall, dark stranger is wearing nothing but a pair of skimpy swimming trunks and boots befitting of the Frankenstein monster.

"What would you like? I can look in the crystal ball or perhaps read your palm?"

Ernie stuffs the remaining chips in his mouth and juts his hand forward.

"Palm." Pieces of chips fly from his mouth. "Sorry about that," he apologises.

She takes his hand and studies his palm. She already has some spiel to lay on him but before she can utter a word she sees something she's heard of but never in a lifetime thought to see.

"God help you," she whispers and collapses back into her rocking chair. She lets his hand drop from hers.

"Sorry, lady, I've been eating fish and chips I'll wash them and..."

"It's not the state of your hand, my love. Who do you travel with?"

Ernie shifts nervously. "Me mates."

"And these, mates! Where are they now?"

Ernie frowns and scratches his head.

"At the beach, why?"

"Go, bring them here to me immediately."

"I'll try but how much you gonna charge?"

Madam Kazel shakes her head and makes the sign of the cross.

"There is no charge. Please go bring them. Be quick be swift."

Ernie looks confused, but he leaves. He goes and swiftly buys a toffee apple and then some hot donuts.

He walks back towards the beach, stopping only to look at the opening times of a curry house.

He spots the others in the distance and makes his way towards them. He greets them and settles into his chair where he promptly falls asleep with his hand jammed down the front of his trunks. An hour later he awakes and remembers to tell them of the curry house and the strange encounter with Madam Kazel.

"You say she never charged you?" Scarlett asks.

"Yeah, she just looked all worried and insisted I bring you lot to see her."

"Ewww, sounds spooky," Sara playfully injects. "Shall we go? Will you protect me, Chris?" She reaches out and grabs Chris's hand.

Gary and Tommy smile, Len giggles loudly.

"What's so funny, Lennard," barks Chris. Sara still holds his hand, Chris starts to blush.

"You couldn't protect yourself let alone anyone else." He throws sand in Chris's direction, Scarlett smiles and taps his shoulder, Len turns to face her.

"You can protect me," she states. "The powers of the unknown are calling us," Scarlett bursts into laughter, Chris grins and the others shake their heads as Scarlett now grabs Len's hand.

"In view of the strange activity going on here, I think it's probably for the best," says Gary looking at Len and Scarlett.

They all get up, brush sand off themselves and get dressed... apart from Ernie. He just places his small purse back in his trunks and tells them to follow.

They arrive outside Madam Kazel's. Huddling outside the strangely painted hut, Gary indicates for Ernie to go in.

"Don't bloody why me, just go in and tell her we're here. You've met her so there's less chance of her putting a spell on you."

Chris stares at Gary and sighs. "She's a medium, Gary, not a witch."

"In that case, you go first!"

Chris looks over to Ernie; the missing link was picking his nose and gawping at two fit blondes as they walked past in their bikinis.

"I think Gary's right, Ernest. You'd better go in first and announce we're here."

Turning his attention from the women and wiping his finger on his trunks, Ernie glares at Chris.

"Don't call me, Ernest." He pushes past Len and enters inside.

Madam Kazel, from the dimly lit room, looks up as Ernie appears.

"They are here!" she says softly, a statement not a question.

"Did you see them in your crystal balls?" Ernie asks nervously.

"No… I could hear you all arguing outside the hut, and it's ball not balls, plural. Now, ask them to come forth."

"Oi, Come in."

Madam Kazel jumps as Ernie bellows to his friends.

One by one they step inside until they are all sardined together.

"Good afternoon, Ernie said you wanted to see us," said Chris nervously, stepping forward. He looks to his friends and steps back again,

"I need to see your right hand, all of your right hands," she solemnly replies.

"Good job she's already seen Ernie's. He's had it down his trunks, up his hooter and god knows where else," chuckles Gary.

"This is no laughing matter," snaps Madam Kazel.

Sara steps up first and the rest follow. I could list the names and order of the hand reading but that would be poor and boring of me to do so, it would just be to word count and… oh look I've made loads more words!

She looks at them and her feelings sway from fear to pity. Sighing, Madam Kazel once again falls back in her chair.

"What is it?" asks Scarlett, her face a mask of worriment.

"You have the sign of the reversed Pentagram on your palms."

In unity, they all look at their right hands.

"I can't see nothing," says Len wandering about with his hand in the air.

"You can't see anything because you don't have the gift, but I can, and god be with you."

"But what is it that's wrong? I mean, why say god be with you?" asks Len, still with his hand in the air.

"The mark of the beast is upon you, on all off you."

"Beast!" Sara looks at Chris and winks. Chris pretends not to be nervous but stares at his hand.

"What beast?" Tommy laughs.

"Please, you must go, and god have mercy on you."

"I don't like this," Scarlett grabs Len's arm.

"What the bloody hell are you going on about, pentangles and beasts?" shouts Gary.

"You are all staying in a place named Drarkland, is that correct?"

"Yeah, so?" replies Gary.

"A terrible curse has returned to the village, a curse that has marked you all for... please, just go."

"You're mad," Tommy pushes his way out the hut.

"Yeah, I agree, mark of the beast." Gary follows.

Ernie farts and moans, Len indicates for Scarlett and Sara to go, Chris bites his bottom lip and leans forward.

"Errr, what sort of beast is it?"

"It is an abomination, born of man or woman and wolf... It will kill you all." Her words, it will kill you all, fills his veins with ice.

"Please, you must go now."

"Are you sure you ain't made a mistake?" Len worriedly asks.

"No... I see all."

They all leave, go back to the beach to get their things and Ernie gets dressed and they walk to a nearby pub.

Madam Kazel is visited by a group of Welsh holiday makers. She makes a tidy sum and they even tip her for her good news, apart from the bloke who she informs will be hit by a strange object. She shuts up early.

Leaving her mystical hut, she walks down the promenade.

In the sky, a gull flies high. Veering off from the sea, it flies inland and above the pier. Its head suddenly clouds over, dizzy, it drops from the air.

Madam Kazel is halfway towards the main stretch. Death and wolves consume her thoughts and then it hits her. She falls to the floor. The sudden surprise and impact cause her to pass out. A gull has plummeted from the sky and has hit her straight on the head. She's out cold… shame she didn't see that in her crystal ball.

The bright and sunny seaside bar doesn't offer much cheer to some of the group. As they sit and nurse their drinks, they talk over the strange encounter with Madam Kazel.

"She said it will kill us," Chris states nervously sipping his fizzy orange through a straw.

Sara and Scarlett look terrified. Gary laughs.

"She's just a nutcase. Bloody hand signs and monsters, she's just out to make a dodgy buck!"

"No, she never charged us, so she must be on the level," Len protests.

Gary flaps his arms and sighs.

"Awww, come on. Ain't you sussed it, mate?"

Tommy shakes his head and sniggers.

"You really ain't sussed it, have ya?"

Len looks confusingly at Tommy then Gary.

"Sussed what?"

"Tell him, Tommy." Gary shakes his head and reaches for his pint.

Tommy leans forward and smiles. "Because she forgot to charge us, you twat."

Gary starts to agree then stops.

"No, you idiot, it's not because she forgot to charge us. Look, she tells us we're all brown bread because some creature is gonna kill us and we get all panicky and go back. We tell her to lift the curse and she says she can but it's gonna take time, spells and a huge bundle of poppy to do so. We cough up the readies, she begins her mumbo-jumbo and before you know it we are all saved and she's quid's in... the long game, Len me old mate."

"Bloody hard to believe there's swindlers like that about," comments Chris, then he looks at Gary and frowns. "I want a full refund on that chess computer."

"Yeah alright, we're on holiday so we'll sort it out back home."

Flock of Seagulls try and run while Len tries to get served, Ernie moans as none of the music is metal and Sara cuddles up to Chris... who feels like he wants to run just like a Flock of Seagulls.

After a few drinks things seem to settle down, that is in the world of the supernatural. Sara is still cooing to Chris, Scarlett is feeling tipsy and dances to the Land of Make Believe whilst Gary loses to Tommy at arm wrestling. Ernie, five pints of Guinness in, decides to challenge him... and then it happens!

Iron Maiden blast out of the speakers, the Number of the Beast erupts and Ernie springs into action.

Pissed and pogoing, Ernie knocks Len flying off his chair. Oblivious, he then starts to headbang.

People start to stare, some in amusement, some in fear. Ernie does not stop.

"Yeeeeeeeeeeeeeeeeeeeeeeeeeeeeeeeeaaaaaaaaaaaaaaaaaaaaaaaaaa aaahhhhhhhhhhhhhhhhhhhhhhhhhhhhhhh!."

"The night was black was no use holding back."

It was when the singer's voice shouted yeah (as above), screaming loudly and as you can read, for a long period of time, it happened.

Ernie jumps up strumming his air guitar. He flings his leg out, fast and forcefully and shooting off his foot like a ball leaving a cannon, his boot takes flight.

The group of Welsh holiday makers consist of Madge, her husband, Di, and their friend, Petra, and her husband, Andrew. In their mid-forties, they have decided to come to the peaceful haven of a holiday resort for a quiet week's break.

Andrew has done nothing but moan, moaned he wanted to go to Spain, moaned that is was full of London overspill on their holidays and moaned about the visit to Madam Kazels.

"What a load of bloody rubbish, isn't it!"

"Oh, for god's sake, Andrew. Why you always bloody moaning?" snaps Petra.

"Because all we have met here is cockneys, and that fortune teller was talking nonsense and now this bloody head rattling music comes on."

Now I'm not going to be predictable and bring up Madam Kazel's warning of being hit by a strange object but as the singer got to the end of his lengthy yeh, Andrew was clobbered by Ernie's clod-hopper. He was hit fast he was hit hard and the last thing he remembers was he hit the deck

Six six six the number of the beast
Sacrifice is going on tonight!

"Jesus Christ... I think Ernie's killed someone!"

The others look at Gary as he points to the table at the far end of the pub, then to Ernie as he stands with a look of surprise on his face, and then towards the table again where a woman is now screaming and where there were four, now sit three.

Not sure what to do, Petra continues to scream, Andrew lays unconscious with a large gash across his forehead, Madge tries to calm her whilst Di attends to his friend.

"Andy, Andy, it's me, Di. Can you hear me?"

Andrews eyes flutter open and he stares towards the ceiling.

"What happened, Di? What hit me?" he asks in a shaky voice. "Oh, my head," he winces and closes his eyes.

I'm coming back, I will return
And I'll possess your body and I'll make you burn
I have the fire, I have the force

I have the power to make my evil take its course.

"Has anyone seen my shoe?"

The group of Welsh holiday makers turn and stare at the strange looking man and then…

…and then I would like to say they handed him his weapon of mass destruction and all had a jolly good laugh at the course of unfortunate events. However, that is not what happened.

Petra stops screaming at Andrew and begins swearing at Ernie.

Madge picks up his boot and throws it at him and Di stops attending to his fallen friend and attacks him.

They leave the pub and head towards the Indian restaurant as Andrew is carted off in the ambulance. There were enough witnesses to say Ernie did not in malice, launch the boot at them but they were told never to come back.

Chris apologises, Len takes the ladies outside, Tommy stops Di from attacking Ernie and Gary is laughing so much he has lost his breath, hurt his ribs and collapsed to his knees.

The Jewel of India sits between a newsagent and a tool hire shop.

They go to the door, Gary is still laughing and pointing at Ernie. Ernie has fallen into a deep sulk and has the face of a hairy boxing glove.

Chris, always the gent, holds the door open for the ladies and then his sandal buckles rattle as he follows them in.

Tommy barks at Gary to shut up… "Or we ain't gonna be allowed in here either." He pushes Len inside now that Len's started giggling too.

Walking into the Jewel of India was like walking into the Taj Mahal itself, nor, thought Len, had he ever been there.

The walls are painted in deep plum and bright gold colours, statues of elephants adorned with jewels stand on either side of the silver-clad bar. Looking in the restaurant itself rows of neatly-dressed tables resided. Above, a large bamboo ceiling fan slowly turns, wafting the amazing smells of onion, garlic and spice towards their nostrils.

There is a white draped curtain swathed across a doorway and from it steps a tall thin Indian gentleman dressed smartly in midnight blue trousers and a waistcoat. His crisp white shirt homes a velvet blue bow tie. His hair is regally swept back. Courteously, he nods and welcomes them.

"Table for seven, please, Gunga Din."

Chris closes his eyes, Sara looks sternly at Gary and turns to Gung… to the waiter.

"Good evening, we'd like a table for seven, please," she states.

"Follow me, please."

They follow him, and they are led to a long table. There are already people dining and soft music begins to play.

"Please," he offers them to take a seat, making sure he pulls the chairs out for the two ladies.

Three other waiters begin to mill about; the Jewel of India seems to be bigger on the inside than it is the out.

They take their places and order some drinks; the waiter shortly returns with a tray of beverages and seven menus.

Among the Masalas, Madrasa's and Balti's in the chief's special section, Ernie spots something.

"The Wrath of Khan." His words are merely a whisper, but they are heard. The waiter's face nears his.

"That, my friend, is a very magical and dangerous dish." He smiles, displaying bright white teeth.

The Jewel of India, fine Indian cuisine.
Chief Specials.
No. 66 The Wrath of Khan.

"Dare you enter a mystical experience of heat and delicious fury?"

The Wrath of Khan is a chicken, lamb or prawn curry infused with spices from Naraka and seasoned in our own house special masala. Served with pilau rice, it is a dish for only the bravest or foolhardy adventurers.

"Has anyone ever tried it?" Chris asks nervously.

"Oh yes, some have tried." The waiter's smile broadens even more.

"And have they managed to eat it?" enquires Scarlett.

Laughter slowly leaves his lips as he places some napkins onto the table.

"Never! The Wrath of Khan is a curry that has never been finished."

"So, what's so dangerous and magical about it?" laughs Ernie.

"The danger comes from the Naraka spices; the magic is to survive but a few mouthfuls. It is written that whoever eats and finishes the Wrath of Khan, their main meal and all the main meals in their group shall be free of charge."

Everyone in silence looks at each other.

"Where is it written in a prophecy?" asks Len... he puts his hand in the air.

The waiter carefully takes a menu and walks towards him. Len swallows and tries to melt into his seat.

"No!" The waiter suddenly stabs at the bottom of the menu. "The manager, Mr Allie, wrote it to let the customer know, should you finish it then you guys eat free."

Gary looks across and smiles at Len. "You wally!"

"I'll have it," Ernie solemnly declares, casually tossing the menu on the table and crossing his arms.

The waiter suddenly and swiftly twists towards him, almost serpent like. Pen and pad in hand, he grins.

"Chicken, lamb, prawn or would you like the vegetarian option?" A sinister grin plays along his face accompanied by an even more sinister laugh.

The challenge has been set and is as follows:

Ernie is to attempt to eat a Chicken Tikka Wrath of Khan served on a bed of pilau rice.

He must eat the entire contents on his plate, including rice, to win the challenge.

He can drink as much as he likes and can stop for a break no longer than five minutes.

He is not allowed at any time to leave the table. To do so forfeits the challenge and the house wins.

If the meal is fully consumed, then and only then, do the rest of the party eat for free. Mains only, no side dishes, any beverages or deserts are included.

Lastly, a disclaimer must be signed agreeing that injury or death is in no way the responsibility of the house.

...Ernie agrees and signs.

"By the way, spices from Naraka, where's Naraka?" Ernie asks.

Leaning into him once again, the waiter's smile shifts to that of a grimace.

"Naraka, my friend, is another name for hell."

And so, the evening gets underway as does Ernie with his curry. He sits and waits and soon it arrives. Already plated, there is a film of heat rising from the dish.

As well as his friends, a few of the other diners come to watch as do the waiters, the chef and the manager himself, Mr Allie.

…And so, it begins!

OK, let's not dwell on the madness that is to commence. Let's just say that after the first mouthful Ernie thought his mouth was melting and after the second he was going into cardiac arrest.

By the fifth mouthful the intense heat had driven him mad. By the tenth it had driven him sane. His mind closes and an out of body experience occurs. On returning to his solid form, he discoveres he is soaked in sweat and it is then that he realises he's eaten the last morsel.

The waiters make a sacred and holy sign towards him as does the chef. The manager curses realising he is going to lose a shit load of money all thanks to the hideous buffoon that sits with glowing red lips.

Strangers pat his back, shake his hand and one person even plants a kiss on his cheek. To be fair, the man was pissed.

His friends cheer and place their orders, Ernie slouches in his chair and awaits his fate... and then he spots the trays of poppadums!

"Bring me some of them, mate! And some dips too."

Ron Ayelsworth's bottle of scrumpy slips from his already loose grip and clanks to the ground. Stirring, he opens his eyes. For a while Ron stays where his is, stretched out in his garden chair and then he notices the daylight has slowly, almost nearly gone.

Ron's been drinking even more than usual since he retired as the village handyman and since has either spent his time drinking with his friend, Beckett, at the Black Crow or getting drunk in the Sheep's Head. Today with his home-made cider, he has tanked up and fallen asleep or to be more accurate, passed out in his own backyard.

He pushes himself into a sitting position and rubs his face. "Crashed out bloody pissed again," he thinks as he widens his arms and yawns.

Was it a snap of sticks underfoot or was it his imagination?

He looks to the bushes that engulf the left part of his garden and stretch towards the forest.

He slowly, on unsteady legs, gets to his feet.

The warm summer breeze blows and the rushes near his pond sway. At the very end of his garden he notices his house is in complete darkness and there is no other reason for it to not be, but something doesn't feel right.

The breeze stops. The night's stillness becomes a loud scream of tense silence.

He places a hand on the garden chair and slowly gazes around. Seeing nothing but the bushes, the pond the house and the path that leads to his back door, he staggers towards it.

Laughter, he hears laughter. It's soft, but he hears it and he stops. He freezes. With wide eyes open he looks towards the house and has a sudden feeling he will never enter his home again.

The laughter grows louder, was it the edge of a snarl? His shoulders tense, sweat breaks on his brow, tingling sensations seep into his face… he waits, the laughter nears him. Powerless and paralysed to move he glances now at the moon and he understands his situation.

The scream he hears ignites him into action and he races towards the house. He realises as he gets closer the scream is coming from his own mouth. The laughter, the shouts, the growls, snarls, crying, swearing, they come, however, from behind him… the guttural roar twists into a guttural laugh. As he falls through an open back door and crashes to the floor, he can't help but look to see what's nearly upon him, but there's nothing, just a summer breeze drifting through the night.

"Oh God, please, please let it leave me in peace."

He stares at the kitchen door and considers his actions; close it, close and bolt it now. But if he moves it will strike, it's out there in his garden waiting, playing, tormenting him.

...Moments pass, the night has fully come. He makes his choice, scuttles to his feet and launches himself towards the door. He slams it shut and shifts the bolt across the top. He would be wiser not to look through the door's window into the garden, but he must... he needs to, so he does.

"Nothing, nothing there."

His voice, like his body, shakes.

From beyond the garden in the forest, something looks towards the house and the drunken old man staring from the window. Its eyes focused and wide, its mouth grinning slowly releases a soft comical laugh. The laugh deepens and becomes a painful growl. It turns and dashes off into the forest.

"Why?" Chris asks also in despair.

"Because there ain't enough room in Sara's motor now that we're all going in it so Ernie travels back with you."

Ernie glares savagely at Gary. "What's wrong with me, Taylor?"

"What's wrong? Bloody hell, mate, you're like a human time bomb, son. If you go off after that ruby you ate, we're all gone for a burton. You go with Chris. That way it's only two people that have to suffer your arse and die when you humanly combust."

Scarlett starts to laugh, and Len starts to fall in love. Tonight maybe, back at the B&B, he can get some time with her! Sara, however, releases a sigh of pity.

"Oh, poor Chris, it's a brave thing you do, you're such a hero."

"Hero, my arse. He's not slaying a flipping dragon, woman. He's just giving me a lift back." Ernie's lips are still glowing red.

"Not so much of it, you," Chris prods Ernie in the arm. "Now get in before I leave you here."

Grizzling, Ernie gets in, as does Chris who is making the sign of the cross.

On bare feet, it rushes deeper into the forest. A loud burst of laughter and it stumbles, naked, tearing at its own flesh as it rolls along the forest bed, spasming and screeching.

It stops still. It lays on its back, arms and legs bunched, its head lifted forwards with its oversized tongue lolling to one side. It would look comical if it didn't look so grotesquely fantastical. It releases a snarl.

Slaver mixed with blood drips from teeth too large for such a small mouth but then the mouth enlarges, not so much a mouth now but a muzzle. The snout stretches and the snarl has become a crazed scream.

Nails grow, peeling the skin from thickening cuticles, hair sprouts from various parts of its body and muscle forms in large mass.

Turning to lay on its front the change continues until the werewolf is complete.

The night had eventually settled. As the cars near Drarkland, Chris fights to control the car as the howl suddenly fills the air.

"Aaaaaaaaaghhhhhhh."

Chris looks at his companion and wonders what the bloody hell's happening.

"OH, MY GOD I'M ON FIRE."

Ernie continues to howl and scream, grasping his stomach and looking upon Chris with red glowing lips and pain-filled eyes, he begs for help.

"W-w-what shall I do? What's happening?"

"Aghhh, it's the Wrath of Khan. It's getting me, quick pull over. The Wrath's nearly here. My bowels are going to erupt."

"I'm not pulling over. Wait till we get back."

"PULL OVER! Either that or I'm gonna shit in your motor and probably over you. AAAAAGHHHHH, IT'S COMING."

Chris's face is flushed with panic. He hits the brake and Ernie flies out towards the bushes, still howling.

It is moments away from the noise. It senses something large is near and the howl told it what it needed to know; it moves towards its prey.

Ernie makes it to the edge of the bushes; he performs an odd dance as he loosens his jeans and pulls down his pants. Chris tries not to look but fascination compels him.

The beast has moved quickly and is now feet away from its kill. Lowering itself, it moves into attack mode.

Ernie, free of undergarments, bends forward and positions his bottom into the bushes. Chris with all his strength tries not to stare but some force of evil makes him continue to look upon the strange ritual being performed before him.

The beast moves forward on instinct and sees a full moon it has never seen before.

There is a sudden pull of silence, a stillness and then a full release followed by a clap of thunder and a raspberry-type rattle.

The brown-type matter is a consistency of solids and liquid. It thunders and lands directly in the face of its attacker. As Ernie releases a scream of relief, the werewolf releases a scream of pain.

Startled, Ernie glances over his shoulder. He sees the creature rolling backwards clawing at its muzzle.

"THE BEAST!," he leaps up and with trousers and pants around his ankles, shuffles at an incredibly amazing speed towards the car.

Chris freezes at the sight before him and sits in shock as Ernie, bare-arsed, sits himself in the passenger seat, the smell as terrifying as the vision.

Crashing backwards, the werewolf hits a tree and for a moment is stunned, then the pain returns.

The brown acid burns into its face, fire… liquid fire, its instincts tell it to find water and it senses home. It bursts into a large clearing and under the full moon across a field, it runs upright, faster than any athlete and then suddenly it drops to all fours and continues faster than any animal on earth.

The pool is soon found. With no hesitation it plunges its entire top half into and under the cool water… relief.

It slowly draws itself away from the pond. Water rolls from its face. It gazes into the pool until it becomes still, staring at its reflection. It suddenly raises its head to the sky. With eyes filled with hate, it looks at the moon, snarls loudly… it thinks of Ernie.

"What the hell's going on?" screams Chris.

"JUST DRIVE!"

Chris puts his foot down and they screech away.

Back at the Black Crow the others sit in the lounge and settle down with some night caps, Sara relieved at last, for a G & T with ice.

"Oh, that's hit the spot! Chris is taking his time."

She flops into an armchair and removes her sandals.

Gary hands Tommy a beer and smiles; Chris has got his work cut out here he thinks. He looks over to where Len sits on the sofa. Scarlett has her arm slung over his friend's shoulder; she's tipsy and giggles… she plants a kiss on his cheek. Len smiles like a Cheshire cat.

The front door crashes open. They hear exchanges between Chris and Ernie, their voices becoming louder as they near the lounge.

As they arrive inside, Ernie is doing his trousers up and talking about a beast, while Chris is angrily telling him he will clean any mess left on the passenger seat up. As you can imagine, this conversation injects some very worrying thoughts into the group's minds.

"What the bloody hell you two been doing?" asks Gary.

"There's a beast," Ernie answers.

Gary looks downwards to where Ernie is finishing buckling his belt.

"A beast! Where?" he worriedly questions.

Ernie begins to explain what's happened. They wince when he, in detail, tells them of the poo hitting the creature's face.

Sara pours herself another G & T, this time an extra large one. Tommy laughs uncontrollably while Len and Scarlett look worryingly at each other.

"The mark of the beast," Len holds his hand out. "The fortune-teller said it will kill us all."

"I saw it," Ernie solemnly states.

Chris begins to feel uneasy and grabs a can of beer from the table. He turns and with a troubled look asks Ernie if it could have been a stray dog.

"NO! It was not of this earth." Ernie recaps the encounter, a glazed expression crosses his face. "It was like the old women said, of Man and Wolf. It was huge and covered in patchy fur and its face... oh god, its face," he pauses and gets himself a drink... silence.

"Well?"

Ernie looks at Gary. "Well what?"

Gary frowns, scratches his head and walks nearer to Ernie.

"Well, what was its bloody face like, you tit?"

"It was horrible, weren't it," Ernie offendedly replies.

"Yes, but what was it like, Ernie?" asks Len, standing up.

"It was not of this earth," he whispers, causing Gary to throw his arms up in despair.

"Listen, you twit, what did its face actually look like? And if you reply with… It's not of this earth again or it's horrible, I'm gonna kick you straight in the bollocks," threatens Tommy.

Ernie pulls a face, the face he always pulls when he's about to drop into a major sulk and he feels a sudden burning sensation growing in his stomach.

"It looked like a person with its faced misshapen into that of a wolf's. It had long sharp teeth and its eyes glowed with different colours the rest of its boat was covered in shit… I got to go to the bog, it's back, the Wrath is back."

Ernie barges past Gary sending him crashing onto the sofa and rushes out into the hallway. There is a colossus stomping sound as he ascends the stairs followed by the slamming of a door and a distant howl of pain.

"He's bleedin' crazy," mumbles Tommy.

"He was in a right state, though," Chris warns. "He moved like lightning out of those bushes. Never seen anyone so frightened."

"And you never saw this beast?"

Chris looks at Scarlett and shakes his head.

"No, unless you include Ernie!"

"But it is dark, he may have made a mistake," Sara informs them.

"Yeah, but look at the size of that moon," Gary points outside into the night's sky. "And look how bright it is."

"And if this beast is a werewolf, well, aren't they supposed to come out during the full moon," Len's voice is trembling, Scarlett grabs his hand tightly and he sits down.

Chris can't believe his luck; a quiet week in the country is being turned into seven days of chaos and mayhem. He makes a strange shrill sound and downs his beer. Immediately he reaches for another one.

"Thirsty son?" laughs Gary.

Chris takes a huge gulp and slams the can down.

"No, but if I drink enough, I might forget that I've got a man-eating monster after me and that Ernie has left skid marks in my passenger's seat. That I've been sold a dud chess computer and that someone's been taken to casualty because they've been hit with a flying shoe." His head despairingly flops into his hand and he sits down.

Sara crosses the room and puts her arm around him.

"It's OK, Chris... I'm here." She moves her hand to the side of his face and pushes it against her ample bosom.

"So, what do we do?" Len asks, looking around the room.

"Nothing to do," laughs Tommy. "Look, some woman goes and tells us we're gonna get killed by a beast, Ernie pissed up unloads his guts in a country lane and some creature unfortunately gets covered in it... turn it in! If you lot want to believe there's a monster charging around the countryside covered in Ernie's cack, then that's up to you. As for me, I'm having another beer and then I'm hitting the sack."

"Maybe Ernie saw his own reflection," Len hopefully cheers.

"How the bloody hell does he see his own reflection? He's in some bushes taking a pony... where the bloody hell does the mirror come from? I think Tommy's right... however, there's another angle to all this!"

"Oh god, here we go," moans Chris.

Gary stands centre in the lounge, his finger resting on his chin.

"Say somehow the fortune-teller could see the supernatural and say that was a creature of darkness hiding in the bushes readying itself to pounce on Ernie and drink his blood, you know what it could mean...?"

"What?" Sara softly asks.

"It means we could earn ourselves a fortune."

"Knew it," mumbles Chris, returning his face to the sanctuary of his hand and away from Sara's boob.

"Alright?" Len nods to Beckett as he wanders into the lounge.

"Yes, thank you. Evening all. Heard some raised voices and wondered if all was OK?"

"Everything's fine. It's just our pal Ernie has the two-bob-bits due to the fact he ate a proper hot curry earlier," Gary explains.

Beckett chuckles and makes his departure. "Oh dear! He'll have ring sting in the morn!"

Chapter Eight
Wednesday

Gary walks towards the shop, Tommy is still snoring off last night's session in his bed and Chris, Len and the two women are in the garden still discussing last night's events of the unknown… Ernie remains in the toilet with a developing bout of severe ring sting.

He pushes the door of the shop open and steps inside. Tim, Deloris's miserable brother, stands behind the counter. Gary feels his heart drop.

He walks towards the counter and removes his Ray-Bans (imitation ones).

"Twenty JPS please, mate."

Tim turns to reach for the cigarettes. Deloris's voice comes from somewhere behind but it's dark in the hallway and he can't see her.

"Morning, that you, Gary?" she hollers.

"Yeah, you alright, babe?" he shouts back.

Tim places the cigarettes down and without saying anything takes the money… moody looking git, Gary thinks.

"Yeah, I'm fine."

"Oh good. Come out here I can't see you stuck in there." He stares at Tim.

"I can't my (pronounced moi) darling, I'm busy out here stock taking."

"Oh OK, maybe later tonight, aye?"

"I can't tonight I've got plans… tomorrow night though."

Gary feels hope inject itself back in his heart.

"Yeah OK, where abouts tomorrow night?"

"My place, it's just inside the woods up from the Black Crow. I'm out all day tomorrow but meet me at about eight and I'll cook us dinner."

Gary looks at the miserable Tim and grins.

"OK, babe. See you then."

"OK, Gary," she shouts back. He replaces his sunglasses and takes his leave, whistling.

"Catch it and promote it," Scarlett repeats Chris's statement.

"Yup, last thing Gary said to me before going to bed last night."

"But he said it was all a load of rubbish."

Chris looked upon his small friend; he was wearing blue shorts a blue t-shirt and a white Nike baseball cap. He resembled a Smurf.

"That was until he realised that if he can prove the existence of such a thing, he can exploit it and make a fortune. Suddenly, Gary Taylor wants to believe more than anything else this thing is for real."

Chris turns on the radio. Duran Duran are Hungry Like the Wolf… how coincidental. Ernie suddenly appears.

"Ughhh," Chris jumps and as he does his sandal buckles jingle a tune. "Why do you have to appear like that?" he snaps, waving his sunglasses franticly towards Ernie.

"Like what? I'm starving." Ernie has got his entire biker gear on including the leather jacket and is already sweating profusely. He wanders around in the garden, for no real reason, then returns to the small white table where Len and the girls sit. He complains about his sore sphincter.

"My arse hurts, any tea in the pot?," he asks.

Tommy now enters the garden, he looks at Ernie and shakes his head.

"Morning Tommy," greets Chris. "You're up early, well, for you anyway."

Tommy leans over the table and shares morning salutations with the ladies. He grabs a cup and snatches the tea pot from Ernie.

"Thanks to that plank flushing the bog over again and again." He points at Ernie. Gary now steps into the garden. "And that git shouting wake up tosser in my ear, I ain't got much choice but to get up."

Gary laughs. "Did I say that? I thought I said good morning Tommy as I left the room."

Tommy growls. Like his patience, the tea's nearly run out.

"I'm going to make a brew. I just saw the old fella and the woman who cooks, so breakfast shouldn't be too long."

Gary grins and rubs his friend's head as he walks past him. Stretching his arms and lifting his face to the sun-filled sky, he spins around and continues to grin. Chris feels worried. When

Gary Taylor is in a good mood it usually means some poor sod's going to suffer.

"Chris," Sara, who is wearing an orange dress that seems to blend with her hair, taps his shoulder.

"Yes," Chris is wearing one of his hideous floral shirts. Sara for god only knows why, thinks he looks fantastic in it.

"I was thinking of driving back to Hurlsworth Bay today and I wondered if you would like to come?"

"Why?" his voice was tinged with a slight panic.

"Well, I spoke to Scarlett and she also thought it might be nice if you and I and she and Len came. We could have something nice at the fish restaurant a stroll along the beach... I thought it might also be an idea to see the fortune-teller again."

"Why?" This time his voice was filled with complete panic.

Sara touches his arm. "To try and get some closure on this nonsense. It's wrong of her to say such things like we are going to be killed and with Ernie thinking he saw it last night, it's tainting the time we have here."

"Didn't think... saw it," states Ernie.

"Nevertheless, it wouldn't hurt to have a quick chat with her and we can have another more peaceful day at the seaside." She tries not to look at Ernie; Ernie doesn't care. He smells bacon; he heads towards the breakfast room.

"I'm up for it." The Smurf slings his arm around Scarlett's shoulder.

Gary still can't believe the jammy little sod's pulled her.

"Gary, if you and the others would like to come."

He looks from Scarlett and smiles at Sara.

"No, listen, you lot have some time by yourselves. I think Tommy and Ernie want to do a spot of fishing and there's a river near the woods, so I might relax there with them and have a liquid lunch in the tavern."

Relief fills her. She's glad to spend time with Chris without his friends causing mayhem.

Chris sighs. He's not keen on visiting the mad medium again and he has concerns over Sara's advances towards him. Still, it would be a time out from the others and Len can't cause much tomfoolery if he's with Scarlett.

"No, you're not bringing that instrument of damnation and I don't care if you stand and scream again."

They've had their breakfasts and are packing their swimming costumes. Len stands inside the bedroom, the camera in his hand.

"But why? I can get a nice picture," he protests.

Chris moves towards him. Removing the fearsome object from Len's grasp he places it back in the corner of the room. Turning, he places a hand firmly on Len's shoulder.

"Listen, Lennard, I'm a bit worried about seeing this medium again. I'm having reservations about Sara's feelings of friendship towards me and although the others aren't there to cause chaos, that still leaves you, and reflecting on previous events you're still quite apt in that department... so no, no, you can't bring that thing." He points an accusing finger in its direction.

Len shrugs and looks up at him confusingly.

"What do you mean reservations about her feelings of friendship?"

Chris looks shiftily around himself and lowers his face closer to Len's.

"I think, I think she wants to be more than a friend... I think she wants to ravish me."

Len laughs, Chris looks petrified.

The drive through the village is so picturesque, thinks Chris as he starts to relax in the passenger seat of Sara's car. I have, earlier in the story, described parts of the village in brief yet I fear I have not done it justice and as the sunshine highlights its beauty I do not think my descriptive writing could.

Let us then look to programs like Emmerdale and Midsummer, it's a bit like them but better.

Sara turns on the radio. Bonnie Tyler sings about Heroes. She smiles at Chris and comments on having hers already. This causes Len to laugh. Scarlett, who is dressed in a pink denim dress looks tanned and radiant, playfully taps his knee and tells him not to be mean, Chris forces a smile... he really does look like a guinea pig with mop hair.

Ernie finally gives in and removes his jacket. They lay stretched out in the garden. Gary and Tommy just wearing shorts, talk about the upcoming football season. Tommy's playing his UB40 cassette.

"This is shit music," moans Ernie.

"No, it isn't, it's better than that headbanging rubbish you listen to," Tommy argues.

Ernie gets up from his sun lounger and stretches.

"I'm getting some beers from the shops."

Gary and Tommy smile.

"Good man, Ernie. Make sure they're cold," says Gary as he lights a cigarette.

Ernie nods and walks towards the ghetto blaster.

"Shit music." He kicks it over and runs before Tommy can get up. Gary chuckles as Tommy threatens to batter him and calls him Oddbod.

"So, what do you make of all this monster business?" asks Gary as Tommy gets up and places his Brixton briefcase upright.

"I think it's a load of cobbler's, son! How the bleeding hell can some batty old bird look at our hands and think we're all gonna be killed by a beast. Listen, you were right when you said about trying to play the long game... and you're right, she'll charge Chris and co a fortune today, you wait and see."

He mumbles something about Ernie being illegitimate and flops back onto the lounger.

"So, what about what happened to Ernie?"

"Don't know! It must have been some animal wandering around from the forest. I mean, let's think about this... do you really, honestly think that a werewolf or whatever it was tried to attack Ernie and got shit on for its troubles. It's bloody madness, mate."

Gary releases a trail of smoke and sighs.

"Suppose. Shame though, last night I was all fired up for capturing it. Imagine the poppy (poppy red-bread-bread and honey-money) we could make having something like that. Probably get a film out of it. They could get one of those handsome Hollywood actors to play me; Richard Gere or some mush like him. Could have got a book deal too. Bloody hell, I could be rich!"

Tommy leans on his elbow and stares at him.

"I mean, we could be rich."

"Richard Gere, you plumb! Listen Gary, one it's all bollocks and two… you're mad in the bleeding head, son."

"Alright, ya mouthy git! But just say it was real! Maybe we could say Ernie is some type of beast?"

Tommy laughs as does Gary.

"Ernie Smith, half man half stain," bellows Tommy and they continue to cackle.

The bell rings in the general store. Tim, who has had to pop upstairs has been replaced by Deloris. Looking up from her magazine she smiles at the large, ape-type figure that enters her shop.

"Morning," she greets him with a smile. Ernie stops and stares at her. "Lovely day, isn't it?"

He says nothing and just continues gawping.

Deloris wonders if there's something wrong with him; Ernie is frozen.

"Ernie," he bleats. Suddenly, he unfreezes himself and walks towards her. The closer he gets the more her beauty radiates and then he notices her eyes; pools of colours swim together.

Deloris smiles again. "Ernie, is that your name?" she giggles.

"Yes," he softly replies. "How did you know?"

"Because you just shouted it out." What a complete idiot she thinks.

"Aye! Oh, yeah, I did." He continues to stare.

"I take it you're staying at the B&B?"

As Ernie starts to gather himself together, Deloris notices a massive stain of jam or sauce on his t-shirt.

"Yes, me and my mates." He shuffles nervously from foot to foot.

"So, do you need any help?"

Ernie makes a scoffing noise and grins. "The question should be, how can I help you?"

"Sorry?"

"Oh, it's just what me mate Chris says when we do staff training. I work in a shop as well."

"I see." She didn't.

"Do you sell beer?"

"In the fridge over there." She points. Ernie doesn't look, he just stares.

"I'm back now." The sudden arrival of her brother jolts Ernie back to the real world. He wanders towards the fridge still turning to look at her. Deloris, relieved by Tim's return, gets up collects her magazine and takes her leave.

Ernie takes the cans of beer to the counter, pays and makes his way back to the Black Crow. All he can think about is the woman; her beautiful faced marred only by what looked like burn marks across her cheeks.

And so, the day continues; morning finishes, the afternoon begins and all the while the sun beats down.

At Hurlsworth Bay, Chris, Sara, Scarlett and Len sit inside a small cave looking out towards the sea that sparkles like a million diamonds. They stretch out on beach towels and discuss where they should go for lunch. Chris pours Sara a glass of sparkling water and himself a glass of sparkling Mateus Rose wine.

Scarlett sits crossed leg and sips a can of coke. Len thinks of his son and how nice it would be to have him here. They haven't seen Madam Kazel yet; they would have lunch then visit... for the time being, all thoughts of darkness are laid to one side.

"This has to be one of the most beautiful views I have ever seen," Chris openly declares.

"Mmmm," is Sara's response as she leans her head on his shoulder.

Chris looks down upon her ginger barnett, what to do?

OK let's cut to the chase. She's not the prettiest bird in the trees and she's carrying a few extra pounds, her hair's bright ginger and Chris is sure he's heard her, on more than one occasion, fart. But she seems to like him and she's a nice person. She's considerate, funny and to be honest the only women to have shown him any interest in a long time. He leans to the side, his face lowers, he pauses then continues... this goes on for some time, and then takes the plunge, throws caution to the wind and gives her a quick peck on the head... unfortunately for Chris, she raises her head to talk to him, as he lowers his... wallop!

Tommy and Ernie sit at the small river bank with their rods dangling in the water. Please, really, behave!

Ernie has used one of the fishing nets to place the beers in and then gently lowers them into the cool water to keep them chilled.

"Wonder how the others are getting on?"

"Don't know, but I do know something. What I saw last night was not of this world."

"Please don't start that pony again. I told you it was probably a fox or something," moans Tommy.

"It was over seven foot, for Christ's sake."

"Then it's a bloody big fox."

"It wasn't, if anything it was more of a bear."

"A bear, in the forest! Ernie don't be such a pranny. That's a stupid thing to say."

"Well, you won't believe I saw a werewolf so what am I supposed to think and say... I'm going for a piss."

Disgruntled, Ernie gets up. Tommy's brought his radio and UB40 are playing, so Ernie once again kicks it over.

"Saw a werewolf," he stubbornly states and walks off.

Tommy sighs, curses and reaches for his radio.

"You'll see bloody stars if you keep doing that."

After last night's unsettling events, Ayelsworth takes solace in more scrumpy. He locked his doors and drank till he fell into a deep sleep; he woke late in the day and continued to drink. He'd staggered out the side gate of his garden and into the woods looking for clues, amazing what a bit of Dutch courage and daylight can do.

He steps unsteadily forward.

Ernie unzips his fly.

Ayelsworth decides to head towards the river; he doesn't even know what sort of clues he's after.

Ernie starts to pee, relief and well, I guess we all know where this is going. Though Ernie didn't piss on Ayelsworth as he staggers into view, he just screams and runs, a torrent of urine splashing everywhere.

"BEAST," he cries. Tommy turns and sees his friend rushing towards him; he holds his willy in one hand and is flapping with the other... Ernie is still peeing.

Aylesworth curiously follows.

"STAND BACK," shouts Tommy as Ernie draws upon him. Tommy rolls to his side, tries to stand and falls to his knee. Ernie, although now in control of his bladder, dives over him, dignity and everything else gone for a burton.

Ayelsworth appears and points with a shaky old finger.

"What do you know of the beast?"

Sara pours a drop of water onto the end of her hanky and presses it softly against Chris's lip.

"It's nearly stopped bleeding now, darling."

Chris lays still with his head on her lap, Len is still laughing uncontrollably, and Scarlett tries hard not to join him.

"What on earth happened?" Scarlett asks.

Before Chris or Sara can answer from and in-between bouts of laughter, Len speaks up.

"I saw it... hahaha... Sara, Sara's head resting on his shoulder and Chris, oh god, hahahaha, Chris bends forward to kiss her and Sara at that precise moment lifts her head up and nuts him! Aghhahhhaha!"

"I'll bloody do you," shouts Chris, wriggling in temper. This must be one of the most embarrassing moments ever and Len was bound to tell Gary and the others, making his life even more miserable.

Sara rests a hand on his chest and tells him to calm down and stay still.

"So, you were going to kiss my head? Oh, Chris how lovely you are."

"OH GOD!" Chris thinks. "She's making it worse."

Len begs for help and rolls about laughing.

"I'll take laughing boy here with me and we'll get a table in the fish restaurant. We'll meet you in there." Scarlett helps lift Len up and brushes the sand off him. She packs up their towels and leads him out of the cave. Len staggers about chuckling loudly, older readers think back to Norman Wisdom and you pretty much have the scene.

Sara removes the hanky the blood has gone. She lowers herself and gently kisses him, making sure she doesn't hurt his injured lip but ensuring she gets her message across.

Tommy nudges Ernie over, gets up and runs towards the tall white-haired old man.

"Come here, you." Angry that he was nearly soaked by Ernie, he grabs Ayelsworth by his shirt and drags him towards his cowering friend.

"Is this the bloody BEAST?" he shouts, ignoring the pleas of Ayelsworth.

Ernie blinks and pulls the look where his lips look like sausages.

"NO! That's not the beast, just some old pisshead by the looks of him."

Tommy lets go and the struggling Ayelsworth falls to the ground and begins to sob.

Ernie gets up and brushes the dirt off himself.

"He startled me, that's all, I'm still spooked from last night," he grumbles. "Good job I decided not to go into attack mode."

Tommy swears at him and turns to the mess that is Ayelsworth.

"Alright, me old mate. It's OK, no harm done. I didn't mean to be rough with ya it's just me and me pal got spooked."

He takes him by the elbow. Ayelsworth with bloodshot eyes looks up.

"But what do you know of the beast?" His words are low, his voice trembles.

So, they explain. They start with their visit to Madam Kazels and with Ernie's encounter. Ernie describes what he saw and Ayelsworth nods.

"Then you had a lucky escape, as did I last night... the beast is back; the Drarkland curse has returned."

Tommy and Ernie look at each other while Ayelsworth explains everything.

Eventually they say farewell to Ayelsworth and promise to keep what he has told them to themselves... apart from telling the others that is.

They pack up their fishing gear and go to find Gary.

As they stroll into the village square, Gary leaves the tavern. He shouts across and waves to them.

Tommy and Ernie put their fishing stuff down and watch as he comes over.

"I've flogged three of them chess computers to the carrot crunchers." He beams. He notices the sombre mood of his pals. "What's up?"

"We need to talk, son. Let's get back to the house and me and Ernie will tell you all about it."

Len and Scarlett both look up as Chris and Sara walk in holding hands.

Chris looks nervous; his bottom lip droops making him look like he's been drugged but really this is what he looks like when he's nervous.

Even before Len can comment, Scarlett elbows him.

"Over here guys." They look over and head towards the table.

The food is fantastic. They have some cocktails, Sara a non-alcoholic one, and then the mood changes.

"Are you sure we should see her?" Len worriedly asks.

"Yes, I'm positive. Like I said earlier today, it's not nice to say the things she said and leave it open without more explanation." Scarlett agrees with Sara.

"OK, in that case, I'll settle the bill and well, settle the score." Chris waves the waitress over and Sara sighs. "How commanding he can be," she thinks, smiling.

Moments later they arrive outside the strangely decorated hut that belongs to Madam Kazel but the door is locked and there is no sign of her.

"Brilliant," Sara moans.

"She's not here."

They turn, a tall pier worker in his oiled dungarees and head scarf smiles, his face a mass of wrinkles.

"Oh, do you know when shell be back?" Sara enquires.

"Don't rightly know. Apparently she had some sort of accident... or so I hear, some sort of animal attacked her."

"Attacked her, when? What sort of animal?" Chris worryingly demands.

"As I say, don't rightly know."

"Who would know?" asks Len.

"The pier manager but he went on holiday today. Won't be back till next week."

"Aw, bloody hell," Chris cries.

The pier worker waves and leaves. The others just stand in silence.

"Who you talking to Gavin?"

The pier worker, Gavin, picks up his tool bag and looks at Freddie, the Dodge car mechanic.

"Oh, just some holiday makers. Told them about Madam Kezal being attacked by an animal."

Freddie laughs, displaying a row of discoloured teeth.

"She wasn't attacked by an animal, you daft bugger! A seagull fell on her head and gave her mild concussion. She's back tomorrow."

Gavin laughs back.

"Oh well, same difference."

Sitting in the bedroom, Tommy pushes the window open. It's stifling now; the day might have moved on, but the heat certainly hadn't.

Gary stands in the corner, Ernie sits in a chair, Tommy cracks open a can of cold beer and begins.

The tale begins a hundred years ago. The village was plagued by a werewolf. The werewolf's identity was revealed to be that of the local cobbler, Simon Tella. Tella had terrorised the village by night, killing livestock and then other villagers. He was discovered and his home burnt with him inside. His remains were buried in the woods and that was that... until now.

No one knows how or why the curse returns but it does. Before Tella there were three werewolves within eighty years of each other, all from different families, all listed as good people, one even a vicar. One didn't receive the curse till she was in her late fifties; the other was a shepherd who butchered his entire flock.

A hundred years later, it's returned.

Gary walks towards the bed and sits down.

"So how does this Ayelsworth bloke know all this and why would he think the werewolf is back?"

Tommy explains it's stories passed down. All the villagers know but they don't like to speak of them, certainly not to outsiders. He tells Gary to keep quiet and not let on, but it would give gravity to what Ernie encountered and to what the fortune-teller said.

"So, it's game on." Gary smiles and punches the air.

"Either that or it's just the mad ramblings of a drunken old man."

"Tommy, I saw what I saw," Ernie pleaded.

"So, what now? Do we pack up and go home?"

Gary looks at Tommy and slowly shakes his head.

"No, we capture it and become rich."

Tommy sighs. There was no point arguing with him.

"But what do we know about werewolves?"

Gary smiles. "We don't but I know a bloke that does, and I know the hotel where he's staying."

"James Austin." They all say his name in unison.

James Austin walks into the reception of the Silver Spring Hotel. It is his third day at the supernatural conference and it feels like his third week... boring was an understatement or boring until he met a rather interesting and beautiful young lady by the name of Sky Sinclair.

He smiles at the receptionist. It's six thirty pm and time for another hour's seminar before the night is over, or looking at Sky, begins!

"Oh, Mr Austin," the receptionist calls to him. He stops and grins.

"Please, call me James."

"I had a phone call for you about an hour ago from a Gary Taylor. I took a message from him and he asked me to pass it on to you."

She hands him the piece of paper.

"Thank you. Sky you carry on and save me a seat next to you at the seminar. I'll be with you shortly."

Sky nods and continues.

Curious as to what Gary could possibly want, he sits in the reception lounge and unfolds the note.

It reads: James, please call this number (the phone number then follows) I can't say much in this note but it's urgent you call.

Please call at eight pm on the dot. I'll be waiting to take your call from the local phone box. I'll wait five minutes. If I don't hear from you I'll take it that you have not yet received this in which case call the number tomorrow at nine am.

Cheers mate, Gary.

James folds up the note and places it inside his suit pocket. He'll go to the seminar on poltergeists and then to his room ready to call his friend at eight on the dot. Amazing, all bloody week, it's been slow and now he's met a fantastic looking bit of crumpet with a posh voice and bloody Gary wants him to bell him!

"I wonder what that bloody idiot's gone and done now?" He makes his way to the seminar and thinks of earlier and Sky.

James and his earlier encounter with Sky!

The Red Lion is only a five-minute walk from the hotel so being the nearest watering hole, it is ideal for James to relax and partake in some much needed acholic beverages. Holding a glass of double Jameson's with ice in one hand and his book "The Life and Times of Lord Carberry, Adventurer, Explorer and All-Round Dandy," in the other, he relaxes into the soft leather chair... That is until his attention is taken by the loud drunken laugh of some idiot in a hideous lime-green tracksuit.

Looking over the top of his book, he raises an eyebrow in distaste as the inebriated fool falls against the bar and cackles. Then he spots her.

She sits at a small round table; the sun shines through the window and highlights her long straight blond hair. She too is reading, and James notices her high cheek bones and perfectly straight nose. She glances up and their eyes suddenly meet; she has pale blue eyes that are simply stunning. She gives a small smile and continues to read.

"What a looker," thinks James as he raises his drink and sips at the smooth whiskey.

His attention is once again pulled by the drunk as he announces to all that he's off for a slash.

He staggers off, scratching his permed barnet. The drunk is short, fat and in his late thirties and James wonders "Why the bleedin' hell they still serving him!"

Sky looks as he wobbles past her. She looks then towards James and realises he's at the convention too. She spotted him earlier in the week and thought then he was quite a nice-looking guy. She returns to her book. Coincidentally, it's the same one that James is reading!

James catches her looking again, then he too realises she's at the convention... wow, what a lot of coincidences.

Oh, I can't be arsed. Let's just cut to the chase otherwise I'm going to keep having to write about them bloody looking at each other and to be fair it's boring and well, to be fair you must be getting bored too! So, dashing forwards a while later the little fat geezer with the crap tracksuit and shit perm stumbles out of the bog and stumbles into her table. He cops an eyeful of a fit blond sort and decides to ask her if she fancies going halves on a bastard? James jumps up and steams over to her table like Ivor the Engine, chest puffed out and everything! But he's too late. The fit blond, who's slim, tall and with a nice pair of pins, leaps up, grabs his curly mop and introduces his head to the table. The drunk is now proper legless. Everyone looks in astonishment, including James. Sky collects her book and handbag to leave.

"Please let me help you."

She looks, and James Austin is by her side, both his charming smile and gold-rim glasses shine in the ray of sunlight that was moments ago upon her.

"Shall we leave together?"

She nods at his suggestion as he motions to the door of the Red Lion.

So, there we go, when James meets Sky. She's twenty-nine and works for an advertising firm in Kensington. She has a very nice voice, a bit like that Joanna Lumley, and a very nice black belt in karate and jiu jitsu, hence the way she dealt with the pisshead earlier. They mention about noticing each other at the convention and both comment on how tiresome it is. Realising they have another hour to kill, they find a local eatery and have a spot of dinner. They discuss the book they are both reading. What a man, they both agree and what a total legend. Sky admits she has a total crush on the book's hero and James tells her he's certainly a great guy and totally gets her crush.

James tells her about himself and she does the same... and to once again cut to the chase, they arrange to go for a drink at the hotel bar after the poltergeist talk.

"Game on!" James thinks and smiles to himself.

"Game over!" when he reads the message from Gary.

...Or is it? At least he's got tonight.

And so, the rest is straightforward. They yawn through the longest two hours ever and then go to the bar. Sky dazzles him with not just her looks but her wit and he wins her over with his smooth Austin chat. He sadly tells her about his pending departure come the morning and she makes his day by giving him *her number to arrange a night out at some point. They spend a nice evening together. James talks about his fascination of the supernatural and Sky tells him that her interests are quite personal and when she gets to know him better she'll explain it all. They have a small bite to eat and a few more drinks. James walks her to her hotel room and gets nothing more than a deep long kiss goodnight. Still, that's fair enough as she ain't that sort of bird and James is quite respectful of that.*

He gets inside his room, takes a cold shower and flops into bed, Sky, however, starts to think of her grandmother and how it was she that gave her the open door into the spirit and supernatural world.

Sky strips off to her underwear and climbs between the crisp, cool sheets. She lays on her back and reaches across to flick the table lamp switch off. As darkness fills the room, thoughts of her grandmother fill her head.

She was eight and her mum's mum, Granny Suzi, was babysitting whilst her dad was at work and her mum at a WI meeting. It was the school holidays and Sky was thinking of her visit to the zoo come the weekend. She looked at her gran who was dozing on the sofa and smiled. She loved her Gran Suzi more than anything. She would let her have sweets when her parents wouldn't, and she would swear when she thought no one was about to hear her. Sky would laugh and cover her mouth as not to be heard... best of all, she would tell her scary but great ghost stories! Her gran was a widower. Her husband, Sky's grandad, Bertie, passed away three years ago. Where her gran had a loud London accent, her grandad's was softer and very, as they would say in the old days, well-to-do. He was involved in politics and came from a money background. Suzi, in her younger days, was involved in bits and pieces that had negotiated themselves of the back of lorries and was born and bred in the Bermondsey area, but opposites do attract and, so they met, fell in love and married.

Suzi woke up, caused by her own snoring. She looked around the living room and then upon her granddaughter.

"Cor blimey, went out like a bloody light I did," she laughed, and sat herself up, looking and smiling at Sky.

Sky looked beyond the wrinkles and years to see the beauty in her gran's face. Her skin was lined, her hair grey but her eyes still sparkled.

"You were bloody snoring, Gran!"

Suzi made a round shape with her mouth and waved her bony finger.

"Don't you let ya bloody mum hear you use that bloody word or I'll get the bloody blame," she cackled and ferreted about in her handbag, Sky giggled and picked up her ham sandwich.

"Your mum learnt to talk proper 'cause ya Grandad Bertie was a toff and ya mum and dad want you to chat all plummy! Now there ain't nothing wrong with that, each to their own but..." Suzi trails off and begins to look confused.

"What's up Gran?" Sky quizzically asks.

"I can't bloody remember what point I was gonna make." She pulled a funny face, chuckled and reached forward to touch her granddaughter's cheek.

"I love you, Sky, with all my heart, always know that."

Sky places her small hand against her gran's.

"I love you too, Gran."

They both look at each other and indeed there is an unconditional deep love.

Suzi stands up and straightens her skirt.

"I'm out of menthol fags, so I'm nipping to the corner shop to grab a pack otherwise I'll be climbing the bleedin' walls. I ain't gonna be no more than five minutes so don't worry, you'll be fine."

"OK, Gran."

And so, Suzi left... and then she returned.

Sky knew her gran was back, even before she entered the room, and the reason? The aroma of menthol cigarettes! That was her gran's smell.

"Hello, Gran. You were quick."

"Told ya I wouldn't be long, didn't I."

Suzi smiled and once again Sky could see the distant beauty of a younger face. Not that her gran wasn't beautiful to her now, it was just as her youth seemed to be shining through today.

"Sky, my angel, can I ask you something?"

Sky, finishing the last morsel of her sandwich, nods.

"The stories I tell ya about ghosts, well, some are scary but darlin' I don't mean to frighten ya and to be truthful some ghost stories can be nice, aye!"

"Yes, Gran. I remember the good ghosts you've told me about."

Suzi smiles and nods.

"Good, that's good my angel 'cause they're the ones I want you to remember."

Nodding, Sky asks if she can switch the telly on.

"You can in a bit, darlin'. I just want to talk with ya a little bit longer before I go."

"Mum isn't back yet so you can't go."

Suzi smiles. Her hair has fallen from its bun and is cascading towards her shoulders.

"What I was saying earlier about the way we talk and all that. Well, what I think I was trying to say was, well, it doesn't matter how you talk but what you say. You can have the voice of an angel but the words of a devil and vice versa! Be yourself and do your best and don't be scared."

The last words, don't be scared, were confusing to her.

"Don't be scared of what Gran?"

Granny Suzi's hair seemed to be less grey and her wrinkles, some of them were fading.

"Just always know how much I love ya, my angel, and your mum. I can hear ya grandad and smell him! I loved that cologne he used to wear."

Before Sky could question any of the odd things her gran was saying, the front door slammed and the living room door burst open. Sky jumped and turned to see her mother rush in. Her mum's face was white, her eyes red with tears running down her face. She bent down and gathered her daughter in her arms to hold her tight whilst she sobbed and mummbled words into her ear.

"Oh, sweetheart. I was on my way home and I saw the ambulance… it's gran, she's…" her mother breaks into a deep sob! "She's had a heart attack outside the shop! My darling, your gran is dead!"

148

Over her mother's shoulder, Sky stares at the beautiful blond young woman that now sits where her gran did. She sees behind her a young handsome man whose hand reaches to touch the woman's hand. The woman smiles and blows a kiss, the young man nods and winks. Sky doesn't feel scared, she realises what has happened and she waves a small goodbye. Suzi looks upon Bertie and her lips part into a wide grin, there is a soft glow of light and then emptiness. Her mother continues to cry as small tears of understanding roll down her daughter's face.

Ernie raises one leg up and farts so loud that Chris jumps as he and the others arrive back.

"Oh God! Do you have to wait for my arrival to do that?" complains Chris.

"We've got some pretty spooky stuff to tell you," Gary quietly informs them.

Chris, Len and the women look at each other and then towards the other three.

"So have we," replies Len, a slight squeak attaching itself to his voice.

They sit in the lounge and speak in hushed tones. Ernie keeps guard on the doorway in case Beckett comes in... for all they knew, he might be the werewolf.

"Anyway, I remembered the hotel where James is, so I left a message for him to call me at the village phone box at eight. Now it's just gone six so hopefully he'll get the message and call."

"Why not get him to call here?" Len asks.

"Because, tiny brain, I don't want Beckett to ear wig. Like we agreed, he might be the werewolf." Gary paces around and pulls out a cigarette. "If he catches an earful, next full moon and we could wake up to find ourselves dead in our own beds!"

Scarlett has brought a large bottle of brandy down from her room and they all have a glass.

The phone rings at eight on the dot.

"Hello."

"Gary, it's me, James. What's up?"

Tommy stands outside, keeping an eye out.

"Mate, what do you know about werewolves?"

"Werewolves!"

There was a brief exchange of words, Gary hangs the phone up and steps outside.

"Well?"

"He's coming up tomorrow afternoon."

They don't leave the Black Crow. Instead they stay together in each other's company, sitting in the lounge drinking and talking of curses and werewolves. Occasionally Beckett would walk in and they would eye him with suspicion but other than that, they keep a low profile.

Apart from when someone finds a Monopoly board and they decide to play a game. It is not long before Ernie throws it and the pieces everywhere.

Chris calls him a bad loser and Gary calls him a twat-faced git.

"Just because I was winning," Gary complains.

"Cheating," shouts Ernie. He shows more displeasure by booting the small silver dog across the room.

And the evening begins again!

Len is snogging the face off Scarlett in the darkest corner of the room, perfectly acceptable behaviour in the eighties, and Tommy decides he's going to call his missus in the morning. He challenges Chris to a game of pool.

Chris chalks his cue and nervously looks at Tommy.

"If this thing is a werewolf what we going to do? How we going to catch it?"

Tommy breaks, pushes his specs back up and shrugs.

"Dunno, son. That's why Gary's called James. He's the boy for this sort of thing."

They both watch as the ball rolls into a pocket.

"I'm stripes," Tommy informs Chris who, without realizing, is still chalking his cue.

Tommy notices the small pile of blue powder mounting up on the side of the pool table.

"Chris, you clot!"

"What?" he snaps, offended at being referred to as a clot.

Tommy indicates with his head towards the mess he's making.

"Oh." Chris stops and pushes his hair from his face. "It's because I'm worried about being savaged."

Tommy missing the shot, curses and looks at his mate then towards Sara whose getting tanked up on the old "Vera Lynn."

"Don't think you got much choice," laughs Tommy.

Chris looks from him to Sara and nervously puffs his chubby cheeks out.

Ayelsworth has done it again. He has fallen asleep/passed out in his garden. The night has fallen and his name is being called.

He sits bolt upright as he did the night before. He hears his name again followed by laughter. It comes from beyond his garden, from the forest it echoes.

This time there is no hesitation and his legs are strong. He leaps up and runs towards the back door... only this time it's locked.

He twists and pushes but it's of no use.

"Good evening, Ron." Beckett steps out of the shadows and smiles.

"Norman, what brings you here?"

Beckett laughs softly but there seems to be no humour injected into it.

"Oh, I just came to see you. Look what big eyes I have."

Ayelsworth thinks what a strange thing to say. He feels uneasy and tries his door again.

"It won't open, Ron. I took the key and locked it from the outside. You didn't hear me because you were asleep but if I was asleep I would have heard it. I hear lots of things, Ron... look what big ears I have." Beckett laughs again; this time there's a strange depth to it.

Ayelsworth moves away, and then suddenly feels someone behind him. Turning quickly, Tobias Wilks is grinning at him.

"Tobias, w-what are doing here as well? Why have you locked my door?" A fearful panic steels his bones, Wilks doesn't reply he just grins, grins with teeth that seem too large and long to belong in his mouth.

"Look what big teeth Tobias has, Ron. Teeth ready to tear the tongue from people who tell our business." Beckett's face begins to twist and beneath, his cheek bones snap.

"Why did you tell?" spits Tobias. He too begins to morph.

"NO, PLEASE." Ayelsworth runs to the top of the garden but is suddenly blocked as a naked Harold Green leaps from the bushes, his old body covered in random tufts of coarse grey hair. Large claws spring from his fingers.

"Why did you tell?" he hisses. Lunging forward, he knocks Ayelsworth to the ground. Screaming, he tries to fight, his fist pounding against Green's chest.

Ayelsworth releases a cry for help with sweat pouring from his every pause. He sits upright in his room the blanket thrown to the floor.

"Oh god, please help me." A nightmare.

His breathing starts to settle and eventually he lays back down. From the darkness in the room it pounces; the last thing Ron Ayelsworth sees are the long white killing teeth and hateful eyes.

Chapter Nine
Thursday Morning

Beckett stops banging on his friend's door and wonders where he could be. He did say he might go to stay with his sister in South Wexted for a few days and as he can't drive, and she can, she must have come and collected him.

"See you later then, Ron," he mumbles.

Tommy and Gary lay in their beds chatting about events.

"You're bloody mad, you are. That's all I'm saying."

Gary listens to Tommy bang on and wishes he'd never told him about tonight's dinner date with Deloris.

"Firstly, we shouldn't split up now we know there's a flipping monster on the loose and secondly, what about Becky?"

"Listen, mate. You don't know what it's like… no man is an island."

"What's that supposed to mean?"

"It means that, well, as it stands, me and her are separated and, so it doesn't count until we get back together."

"If you get back together."

"Even more reason then! If I'm getting dumped I'm gonna get me rocks off tonight."

"Bloody rocks off, you might get your rocks torn off. What if that bird's the werewolf?"

"Oh, have a day off. You ain't seen her, mate. A dog she ain't."

"You know what I mean! Look, I'm giving Jane a bell this morning I'll ask her what Becky's doing; see if she's said anything."

Gary sits up and folds his arms.

"Yeah, OK… but don't mention nothing to Jane about this Deloris sort, she'll grass me up."

"So, you're still going ahead with this dinner date?"

Gary gets out of his bed. He's wearing his daft wicked willy shorts.

"Too bloody right I am, me old mucka'." He pats Tommy's face and disappears into the bathroom.

Chris is standing in front of the shaving mirror. It's the magnified side and he's plucking his nostril hairs.

Wearing the most hideous orange shorts and a lime-green t-shirt, he begins to hum "It Must Be Love" by Madness.

"You're in a good mood considering we're all going to get eaten by a werewolf!" shouts Len as he hunts for his hair gel.

Chris rushes into the bedroom.

"Keep your voice down, turd brain."

"Sorry! But how comes you're in such a good mood?" Len continues.

Chris puts his tweezers on the side and sits down.

"I think it might be because I like Sara. At first, I wasn't so sure, but you know what, Len? Beauty is definitely in the eye of the beholder."

"It must be if she likes you," Len laughs in his high-pitched cackle.

Chris sweeps his hair away from his face.

"Don't be like that. It's hard for me to, to you know, get the courage up to be with someone."

"I'm only joking, mate." Len pats his back. "I feel the same about Scarlett. Can't believe a bird that fit likes me."

Chris looks up from where he sits. "Do you think... do you think these shorts might clash with Sara's hair?"

Scarlett and Sara sit at the breakfast table and await Len and Chris.

"If we do go to South Wexted we had better invite the others," Scarlett suggests.

"Yes, their friend isn't arriving till late afternoon and Wexted is only twenty miles away."

Scarlett sips her tea and begins to spread her toast with marmalade.

"So, missy, you and Chris are an item?" She giggles and bites into her toast.

Sara clasps her hands together. Resting her chin upon them, she smiles.

"He's so different to anyone I've ever known. He seems to have a worldly knowledge and charm about him."

Scarlett chews and swallows. "He does, I agree."

"And judging by the way you and Len were sucking at each other's faces last night, I'd say you'd both hit it off!"

"Len's so sweet, so innocent. I love the way he laughs… just want to eat him up, hahahaha!"

"Now's your chance." Sara indicates to the door of the breakfast room and there stands the worldly Chris… in the horrendous orange shorts and the new addition of attire, white socks and brand new distressed coloured sandals. Next to him Len, sweetly dressed in his Chelsea football kit… male readers, I offer you hope!

"Typical." Tommy slams the phone into its cradle and steps out of the phone box.

He called Jane and there was no answer, just a constant bloody ring. He turns to walk back to the Black Crow when he hears a man's voice shouting.

"Deloris! Oi! You forgot the keys."

He looks across and sees what is from a distance, however, a first division piece of crumpet.

"So that's Deloris."

She walks towards the man, snatching the keys from his hand. She is tall for a woman, at least five seven and that's just in flats. She has endlessly long legs, emphasised by faded denim hot pants.

He can't see her face clearly, but he knows, she's not a moments wasted horror.

Moments Wasted Horror or MWH for short, is a term used mostly in London for time spent eye grazing at what appears to be a proper hot bit of tail, only to find when she turns around it's

157

a proper two and eight. The feelings accrued dashed to the floor leaving the voyeur angry, ashamed and cheated of time spent indulging in deep sexual fantasies… in short, when you stare at a woman from behind that seems totally appealing to find upon her reverse she is pig ugly, elderly or both!

Deloris walks towards the forest, Tommy can't help but stare at her arse… he just wishes it was a closer view.

Gary gets to the bottom of the stairs as Tommy walks into the B&B. Tommy slams him on the shoulder and winks.

"That Deloris bird?"

"Yeah!"

"You'd be mad not to, son. I'm off for a fry up."

Gary confusingly watches as his friend strides to the breakfast table.

They all agree on Wexted, apart from Ernie who, after eating a full English, decides he's going back to bed.

South Wexted is a town surrounded by countryside with access to the motorway. Agriculture is its main source of income but the Town centre, though not thriving, draws in a reasonable trade.

The focal point as you drive in is the church, an impressive Anglo-Saxon building that stands as a beacon for the townsfolk and tourists.

The sun shines down upon locals and travellers milling about. Sara and Chris pull into the carpark.

"Didn't really give this a lot of thought, did we?" announces Gary.

"How do you mean?" Chris responds as he shuts down the engine.

"Well, why have we come here, I mean, why?"

"Because it's a picturesque town of beauty and historic value," Chris explains.

"What's so historic about it?" quizzes Tommy.

Chris pauses to think… "I dunno', the church will be a reference of local knowledge."

"A reference of local knowledge… Bloody hell's bells Chris. We're on holiday, mate, not on a pilgrimage," Gary barks.

"At some point, Gary, we will endeavour to find a pub!" Chris rolls his eyes and gets out the car.

The sudden tearing sound fills the air. Chris pauses; his movement comes to a halt.

Tommy looks at Gary. Gary looks at Chris… Chris gradually turns and looks at the seat of his shorts.

"Gary, can you err, can you help me, please?"

Earlier the remains of Ron Aylesworth lay in his blood-soaked bed. Now they have been, with his bedding collected up and removed, hidden. The walls have been scrubbed and furniture returned to its upright position. Closing the back door, the figure leaves.

Len, Chris and the girls walk across the small stone bridge that arches over the stream of water that runs through South Wexted park. This is after Gary bought him a new and less restraining pair of shorts. Further behind, Gary and Tommy amble along.

"I bet that stupid grin of yours has something to do with that Deloris sort… dirty thoughts, aye Taylor?"

Gary shakes his head.

"Nah, though I can't wait to jump her bones! No, I'm just happy for those two soppy sods, Me and you, we've had our fair share but them, especially Len with that bitch of a misses and bastard of a bloke Keith."

"Yeah, I guess. I was gonna give him a good hiding, but Len told me not to."

Gary smiles and puts his arm around Tommy's broad shoulders.

"You got a heart of gold you have (av), mate. But to be honest, that Scarlett sort's much hotter than his ex and Chris… well, it's just nice he'll get his leg over for once."

Tommy looks at his friend and feels emotional.

"You're a man of beautiful words, you are, Taylor."

"I know mate, I know."

Ernie leaves the shop, cursing. He was hoping that woman would be in there. Instead, her sour-faced brother serves him. He looks at his digital watch; it's nearly eleven thirty. Nothing to do. Then his stomach grumbles and he sees the tavern… pub lunch.

Ernie walks inside. Only a few patrons are there; some big bloke with dark curly hair, the postman and a very informal policeman.

Wilks looks towards him and nods.

"Pint of Snake Bite and a Ploughman's… and two packets of cheese 'n' onion while I'm waiting."

"Snake Bite!" Wilks replies.

Ernie rolls his eyes. "Yes, I told you how to do them the other night; half pint of cider, half pint of lager and a dash of blackcurrant."

"Oh, yeah, I remember now."

The others look up. Wilks pours the Snake Bite and passes the food order onto his wife.

The policeman, a thick-set man with an even thicker moustache, smiles and nods, the postman draws a brief wave and the big bloke just scowls.

Ernie returns a raised head gesture and faces the front of the bar.

"It cheats!"

Ernie turns. The postman is talking to him.

"Do what, postie?"

"The chess computer your friend sold me…it cheats."

Ernie pauses for thought and realises he doesn't really have anything to give thought to.

"Probably because they're crap, mate," is all he can think off to reply with.

"Aye," responds the postie.

"Think you better give him a refund," the large curly-haired man insists.

"Nothing to do with me, mate. He's been flogged a dead horse by my friend, Gary, that's all," Ernie scoffs to himself and watches as the curly-haired bloke gets up. Bloody hell, he's a giant, at least six, six and built like a tank. His thick black eyebrows knit together in temper.

"Don't you give me that," he threatens.

"It's alright, Heath. I'll see his mate, later… sort it out then."

Heath laughs and stares at Ernie, Ernie wishes his friends were with him now. Bloody Gary.

"I don't think so... mate."

Heath walks towards him. As he does, he pushes over a chair. Ernie looks to the policeman, but he's gone. Alone, Ernie knows what's next.

Leaping from his barstool with a swift flowing movement, he grabs the upstart Heath by the throat and with strength filled with fury, dashes him to the floor.

"Stay down, sunshine. You have engaged me in combat and unbeknown to you I am trained in the arts of Kung Fu and I'm a Special Forces agent. Think carefully about your next move; it could be your last," Ernie warns.

"What you say?"

Ernie blinks. The giant called Heath stands before him; reality returns.

"Shut up and sit down."

Both Ernie and Heath look to where the voice comes from. The policeman doesn't even look up from his newspaper.

Heath mumbles some obscenities and returns to his chair. Relieved, Ernie spins around and returns to the bar.

"How long for my grub, mate? My stomach thinks me throat's been cut."

Chris stands at the bar with Tommy and Gary. Len sits discussing his camera with the ladies.

They order some burgers with steak, chips, scampi in a basket, chicken in a basket... and something else in a basket and return with the drinks.

"Food won't be long, ladies, and I took the liberty of ordering some black cherry gateaux for pudding," announces Chris with a smile.

The conversation turns to the beast of Drarkland and the pending arrival of James Austin.

"So, your friend, James, is he quite knowledgeable about the supernatural?" Scarlett enquires.

"James is the expert when it comes to the occult," states Gary as he lights a cigarette.

"Yes, he's always been into the unexplained and supernatural. Even at school he used to bang on about it," added Tommy.

"You all went to the same school, then?"

Chris looks at Sara and nods. "Sadly, yes. Though James was a couple of years older."

Sara sniggers and Gary looks hurt.

"Bloody cheek! I always looked after you at school. No one ever dared bully you, did they?"

Chris sighs and raises his glass.

"No, to be fair no one caused me any harm… you, however, made up for that."

Gary looks at Tommy and Len, open mouthed.

"What about when that fat kid was gonna beat you up after school and Gary pushed him out the window when he heard about it!" announced Len.

"Yes, Len, I do remember. I was the one who broke his fall when he landed upon me from two floors up. I was off school injured for a week and missed the school trip to the history museum."

Sara covers her mouth and Scarlett buries her face, giggling onto Len's shoulder.

"How was I supposed to know you were standing below the bloody window," protests Gary.

"You get no thanks, do ya, son," Tommy chips in.

"No! I bloody don't," replies Gary as he nurses his injured feelings.

"And what about when you sold me that aftershave for the school disco and it made me smell of horses? Ruined my night, that did," Chris shoots him with a pained look, Sara continues to laugh behind her hand. Scarlett's face is still buried in Len's shoulder.

"It was perfectly good aftershave. You must have had a reaction."

"No, mate. It was shit! I bought some as well and it bolloxed my evening up too," growls Tommy.

"And me," injects Len.

Gary flops back in his chair.

"This happened over sixteen years ago!"

"Nevertheles, we're just trying to make a point," states Chris, tapping the table with his finger.

"And what point's that?" cries Gary.

There's a moments silence.

"Dunno! Can't remember now," says Chris as he scratches his head. "Oh, look, food's here." He tucks a paper napkin into the front of his top and grins at the others.

"It's so hard to believe that a creature like this exists," Scarlett softly announces.

The others nod in agreement.

"Though when I was younger, my brother had a fascination for all the horror stuff. I remember him telling me about werewolves, men or women that change into snarling beasts. I remember him telling me that Red Riding Hood was actually a werewolf tale."

"Was it?" Len squeaks.

"Apparently so," Scarlett replies as she dips her scampi into a pot off tartare sauce.

"It makes sense," agrees Sara. As she munches on her quarter pounder, a chunk of beef falls from her mouth and lands in her lap. She retrieves it and stuffs it back in her gob.

"So, what, don't tell me the brat in the red cape was the werewolf?" Gary jokes.

Scarlett raises a smile and shakes her head. "No, but in some versions the… let me tell you the darker version of Little Red Riding Hood." And so she begins, Sara's already done her burger and Len's dropped his chicken leg on the floor. He bends down to get it and upon his attempt to rise back up, whacks his head on the table. The table rocks and half the drinks spill over.

"SHIT! Me head," screams the awkward sod that is Len.

"Awww, BOLLOCKS," roars Tommy as his is one of the spilt beverages.

People look over. Chris shushes them.

"Shush yourself, Chris." Tommy growls.

"Bloody half-head," moans Gary, draining what is left of his pint.

Sara and Scarlett take control and calm them all down. They order some more drinks and Scarlett once again begins the story.

Red Riding Hood leaves her small home in the village and with a large basket containing food and drink, heads towards the forest and the cottage of her grandmother.

Her grandmother has been poorly but the stubborn old lady refuses to leave her home in the woods to stay with her family in the village so, instead, Red Riding has been asked by her mother to take her some supplies.

"Be back before nightfall," her mother warns.

So, off her daughter goes.

She has made it half way to her grandmother's when a tall, dark man wearing a black cloak steps from the bushes and onto the path in front of her.

"Going on a journey?" he enquires in a deep but polite voice.

"Indeed, I am," answers Red Riding, stopping.

The stranger looks towards her basket.

"And where might that be?"

"To visit my sick grandmother."

And so, she tells the stranger everything. Even the part of the forest where her grandmother lives. The stranger nods and bids his leave. Red Riding continues with her journey.

Eventually, she arrives at her grandmother's. The cottage is dark inside and her grandmother's presence is confirmed by her loud snoring in her wooden bed.

Red Riding takes hold of the curtain. Before she can draw it and let in the light, her grandmother's voice sounds.

"Please don't. The light hurts my eyes."

Red Riding releases her hold and navigates towards the bed.

"Oh, poor granny, shall I light a candle?"

"Yes, dear. But light it on the table near the door. That way it won't hurt my eyes."

Red Riding does as she is told and carefully walks over to the table. Taking the candle, she lights it. The light casts a dark shadow across the room towards the bed. She can see the shape of her grandmother huddled underneath the covers.

"Poor Gran. Mother's given me a basket of food and drink for you. Would you care for something?"

"That's very kind of you, dear, but I'm fine for a while. Just come and sit in the chair next to me."

So, she does. She stares at the top of her grandmother's head and slowly, gently lowers the blanket until she can see her face. The candle doesn't give her much clarity but upon lowering the cover she can recognise her poorly grandmother's face. The old lady's eyes open and she smiles.

"Grandmother, your eyes. They seem to be very big."

"All the better to see you in this dimly-lit room my dear."

Red Riding gently sweeps her grandmother's hair from her face. She notices the size of her ears... they seem to be longer!

"Grandmother, your ears. They are so big."

"All the better to hear you, my dear."

Her gran chuckles softly. Her teeth! They are so large.

"Grandmother, your teeth. They are so big."

Her grandmother begins to rise and sits herself up. She focuses on her granddaughter but says nothing.

"The eyes, those eyes are not my grandmothers. The ears too, they are not the ears of my grandmother. The teeth, the long sharp teeth, they are definitely not the teeth that belong to my grandmother."

Red Riding jumps up and moves towards the door, but she freezes when behind her, a loud howl is released. She turns, and before her stands a large wolf.

As the wolf lunges forward, the cottage door crashes open. The dark stranger from the forest leaps in. He holds above him a large, silver-coloured axe. He wields it straight into the neck of the snarling beast.

Red Riding, who has taken cover under the table, recoils in horror as the head of the wolf rolls towards her. She looks away but can't help but look back... the head of the wolf is no longer there; only the head of her grandmother.

The dark stranger bends down and gently takes her hand.

"Come with me, child. I'll take you home."

And so, she did. The stranger is a forest ranger sent by the crown to investigate strange events in the forest.

Rumours of werewolves have been told and it would appear the grandmother for years had been practising the dark arts and had turned herself into one.

Red Riding was taken back to her village and explained to her mother what had happened and what her gran had become.

Scarlett finishes her tale. Chris and Len look shit scared.

"So, you see," she adds. "The grandmother wasn't killed by the wolf... she was the wolf!"

Chris and Len look at each other and then towards Gary.

"And you want us to catch one! Great," Chris sighs as he shakes his head.

As they start their lunch Ernie wanders back to the Black Crow. To his surprise James Austin's gold-coloured Capri is parked up. He's earlier than he said.

As Ernie gets closer to the entrance he can hear James talking to Beckett.

"Oi, Austin!" he calls.

James turns and greets Ernie with a grin.

"Afternoon, Ernest."

James Austin dons a white suit and pale blue t-shirt. With his hair gelled back he looks like an extra from Miami Vice.

"Don't call me Ernest, and why you dressed up like an ice cream salesman?"

James pushes his glasses up and laughs.

"It's called style, sunshine. Something you've yet to discover. Anyway, back to a room. I'd like one single please, Captain."

Beckett looks from Ernie to James and frowns.

"Another one of your lot. Well, I'm sorry to say but were fully booked up" ...Bloody Captain!

"Aye! But I've come all the way up from London."

"Sorry, but there's nothing I can do!"

Ernie scratches his chin. "Hang on, you can't be. I've got a spare bed in my room."

Beckett winces. Damn the beast and his big mouth.

"Oh yes, so you have... it slipped my mind."

James smiles and pulls his wallet from inside his jacket pocket. Suddenly it dawns on him what is happening and with fear increasingly spreading across his face, he slowly turns and stares at Ernie.

"I don't like it any more than you do," snaps Ernie as he and James enter the bedroom.

"Ah god, it already smells of your arse and other evil things in here." He throws his case on the bed and throws open the window.

Ernie mumbles and heads to the bathroom. He slams the door while James hangs his head outside the window. Shortly afterwards strange thunderous noises start to emanate from the bathroom's vicinity and James starts to wish he was back in Peterborough.

"Thanks a bloody bunch, Gary Bleedin' Taylor!"

Gary pats James's Capri and smiles at the others.

"The cavalry has arrived."

They walk into the Black Crow and head into the lounge. James Austin who is sitting on the sofa reading, stands up and greets them.

"And these two lovely ladies are Sara and Scarlett," announces Chris.

James kisses them both on the cheek. He stares at Scarlett and thinks what a sort she is.

"You do realise I've got to share a room with bloody Ernie," moans James as he sits back down.

"Don't worry, he won't mind," laughs Gary.

James looks sternly at his friend and removes his glasses to polish them.

"He might not but I bloody will when his arse fires up. Pardon my French, ladies. I suggest you fill me in on events,

Taylor, before I bleedin' well fill you in for lumbering me with Sasquatch ."

Gary nods and gets Len to guard the door. He sits next to his friend, James, and explains.

James takes in everything he is told and leans forward.

"And you say Ernie shat in its face? Where's the boozer? I need a drink."

Deloris looks at the clock; it's just gone seven. She takes the chicken from the oven and lets it rest on the side. Covering it with a cloth she uncorks a bottle of red wine and makes her way to the living room.

She looks in the mirror and stares at the marks on her face. They've nearly gone. She gently touches them and curses.

James returns from the pub with Tommy and Ernie. Having eaten a plate of steak and chips, he feels better. He enquires over the Gary and Becky situation and Tommy informs him of Gary's latest encounter.

"So that's why he didn't come for a beer. He's too busy getting ponced up to go around some tart's gaff," jokes James.

Tommy nods.

"Proper fit, mate. He's blagged a right sort. She works in that shop over there." He points to the General Store.

Ernie stops, his face creasing like a clenched boxing glove.

"What? Taylor's seeing the bird that works in the shop?" His jealousy getting the better of him.

"Yes, he's off around there tonight. Don't tell me you fancy her too," Tommy laughs and points at the disgruntled Ernest.

"No! She looks like a right witch-faced battle-axe." Ernie marches off whilst James and Tommy look at each other and chuckle.

Ernie stomps into the lounge as Gary makes his way down the stairs. The smell of Paco Rabanne enters the room long before Gary.

"Someone smells nice," Sara shouts playfully.

Gary catches up with his aftershave and smiles.

"How do I look?"

He stands, wearing a pastel pink Lacoste polo shirt and brand-new Levi jeans.

"Like a big poof… and you smell like one, too," barks Ernie.

"Take no notice, Gary. You look handsome," Scarlett comments. She notices Len has got his arms folded and looks displeased.

"Sorry, forgot," she softy mouths into his ear.

"That's OK. It's not your fault… It's that cheating bastard's fault." Len gets up, strides on small legs towards Gary and prods him in the chest.

"Becky's probably sitting alone, feeling alone and missing you." His voice, though squeaky, carries a serious amount of rage… his ears are red and everything!

Gary leans over and clips Ernie across the head.

"Get off," the sulking giant protests.

Chris places an arm on Len's shoulder and guides him away.

"What goes around comes around, Len. Gary in some way will suffer for his attempts to ravish the young lady behind your sister's back, you wait and see."

"Bloody ravish! I'm only going for dinner," Gary says defensively. He considers whacking Ernie's head but doesn't want another half-pound of grease on his mitt.

"Yeah but it's dessert your after, Taylor," shouts Len.

Tommy and James have walked into the lounge.

"What's going on? All this shouting! Can hear you from outside," asks James.

Chris indicates for Len to sit back down. Scarlett takes his hand.

"Nothing much other than Gary being a cheating git."

Gary frowns and waves Chris away.

"I ain't done nothing, Chris, you mouthy sod!"

"Nothing yet! But when the food's been eaten, and the drink starts to flow! When the lights are low, and you gaze into each other's eyes! When hands touch and electricity draws you like two magnets to hug, to kiss to…"

"Yes, I think we get the point, Chris. Bloody hell!" James intervenes.

Gary flaps his hands. "OK. I'll go over, be polite and then come back."

"Aw, bullshit!" squeaks Len.

Gary gives him the two-fingered wave goodbye, pats James on the shoulder and leaves mumbling… "Bloody magnets!"

Deloris stands naked and looks at the tiny black dress hanging up… that one, she thinks, as she reaches and pulls it over and on… no underwear required!

She reapplies some more body spray and shakes her freshly-washed hair into place. Looking out of the window, it's still light but the moon already jockeys for place with the dying sun in the night's sky. Then she spots him! He follows the dirt path from inside the forest and swaggers towards her cabin. She smiles, he looks nice with his spikey-tussled dark hair and stubbled jawline. She looks back to the moon and touches her face.

It was only a short walk once inside the forest, to Deloris's cabin and Gary had no mind to just have dinner and leave but he was not going to stand and argue with that short arse, Len.

Becky, sitting on her own? She was probably out with Jane getting chatted up!

Gary's pace slows as he nears Deloris's home; the cabin is like something out of a picture.

It is huge and built with logs as she had told him. There were flowerbeds carefully and colourfully dotted around the cabin and the path, even a huge tree stump with a large axe blade half buried into it resided outside the front door.

He picks up his pace and is soon at the door... which is open.

"Hello," he shouts from outside not wanting to just walk in.

No reply.

"Deloris!"

Still no answer... he pushes the door open and slowly steps inside.

The inside of the cabin smells of pine and a soft fruity aroma. There is a large open fireplace and next to it sits a rocking chair with a white throw draped across one arm.

The sofa faces the side wall where a large TV stands. Everything else is hard to see as the blinds inside the cabin are closed and the only light on offer are a few candles.

"Deloris, it's me, Gary!" He steps further inside. To his right he spots an oval wooden table.

Looking ahead there is a door, probably leads to the bog or the bedroom, he thinks.

"Deloris, I'm here. You in the karzie?"

He just finishes his sentence when he is taken from behind; claws flash in front of his eyes.

"OK, listen." James closes the lounge door and places a tray of glasses on the pine living room table. Next to them a bucket of ice and various alcoholic drinks. "I've had time to study and think about the possibility of there being a werewolf in Drarkland... and to be honest, we have to be very careful."

They all sit and listen as James begins his lecture on werewolves and lycanthropy.

Facts about werewolves, as put forward by James Austin.

1. Werewolves are dangerous for the simple fact that no sod knows who the werewolf might be... for instance, it could be your own mum.

2. The full moon doesn't have to be out for them to change, though it does sometimes force a change due to it raising the levels of the body's chemistry.

3. The only known way to kill a werewolf is silver or fire.

4. Because they have no recorded images in the world, werewolves are either described as massive wolves or half and halfs, a big bloke covered in fur with hideous twisted features, sort of like Ernie but with a wolfish head.

5. With reference to the above and going on Ernie's account of shitting on one, the type of werewolf they are looking for is a half and half.

6. If bitten, in all legends the victim, if they live will become a werewolf.

7. Though not relevant to any of the above, if they manage to capture a werewolf they will probably become rich and famous.

8. And again not relevant to any of the above, Chris and Len look like they are going to cry.

So, as the night draws in, the group sit, drink and discuss the events and legends of werewolves.

"Let me tell you a tale." James sits forward in the armchair and reaches for his glass of red wine.

Now the night has sealed the day, the moon hangs bloated and high, James begins.

"Hundreds of years ago in Ireland times were harsh and superstition was high. Let me tell you the story of the Huntsman" ...and so he continues.

The Huntsman, who was once a soldier, adventurer and many other things besides, had come home to his small Irish village. It had been years since he had left and upon his return, apart from his family, his childhood sweetheart was there to greet him. At the shores of Kenkillen she stood, her excited blue eyes sparkling like the sea and her long red hair trailing in the wind.

Michael, the Huntsman, leaps from the small rowing boat that has departed from the American vessel, and wades through

*the few feet of water towards her, calling her name "Mary,"
again and again, his voice battling with the wind.*

*As he rushes to her arms, his family join him and after years
of separation they are all together again.*

*As predicted, Michael and Mary are married. They live in
their small cottage on the edge of the Kenkillen forest but times
as I said, were hard and none more than in the forest and the
wolves that inhabited them. With food scarce they grow
unpredictable; livestock killed and taken, the village takes arms
and eventually as the summer arrives the wolves fall back and
are gone, deep back into the forest... or so they thought.*

*It was a beautiful summer's night when the screaming from
the home of Launa Brady was heard.*

*Her husband was wild eyed and holding a pitchfork. Launa
was on her knees wailing and her baby was gone, taken through
an open window and into the forest.*

*The next day, Michael, who was working away in Delanar
county, returns to hear the news and as he sits in the local tavern,
the tales of witches and werewolves are spoken and traded
amongst the local patrons.*

*"Launa Brady was telling us that it was the devil himself
disguised as a monstrous wolf, that reached inside and stole her
child and devoured it in the forest under the light of the moon,"
was one of the stories told and as with the times, a fever pitch of
fear gripped the village and it was with that that the men took up
arms and headed under the light of the full moon to the forest.*

*As Michael stood in his cottage and tied his sheathed knife
against his waist and leg, Mary sat and wept. She begged him not*

to go but Michael who was always one for an adventure, kissed her goodbye and left.

The men split into groups; into the forest they went, Michael broke off and moved with stealth alone and along the forest stream.

In the distance between the trees he see's movement; someone or something crouches and waits. He unsheathes his blade and slowly draws it as he drops to one knee.

For what seems an eternity he is still and then it breaks cover and races towards him.

It starts on foot, a huge half wolf, half human figure, moving at incredible speed and then it drops to all fours and with even greater speed continues, growling and snarling all the time.

Michael stays on one knee, battle trained and brave he keeps his nerve and as the beast lunges with outstretched claws, he swipes upwards and rolls to one side, the razor-sharp silver blade slices the werewolf's left paw clean off.

The beast releases a howl of pain and escapes into the night. Michael takes the severed paw and wraps it in a cloth. He calls to the others who all come running.

"It is a werewolf, as big as a lion but now with one paw missing."

He holds the wrapped paw in the air.

There are a chorus of different voices as they follow Michael out of the forest and into the village. They march to the tavern where drinks are poured and as they lift their first glass, Michael slams down the paw against the bar and unwraps it... what he sees next makes him cold to his soul and breaks his heart... the paw is no longer a paw but a hand, the hand of a woman and on *the finger a wedding ring with tiny Celtic symbols a ring he knows only too well.*

He rushes from the tavern with his head pounding. He runs through the village and heads for his cottage. Bursting through the front door, he sees her laying on the bed. She is naked and sweating with fever... her left hand is missing. In its place a bloody stump. She turns her head and opens her eyes. Tears spill and she tells him he should have stayed. "I would never have left if you'd have stayed," she whispers.

Michael drops to his knees, screams into the night. As Mary howls, her body begins to convulse and change. As her teeth lengthen, Michael once again draws his knife... the villagers gather outside his cottage. He throws open the door and gazes upon them. With tear-filled eyes he lifts the head of his wife, Mary. The beast of their village is no more... as is his life's love.

James lowers his empty wine glass and places it on the table.

"So, you see," he softly says, removing his glasses to polish them, "The werewolf could be your closet friend or loved one."

"Why are you looking at me?" moans Ernie.

The room is only lit by one lamp and shadows seem to dart about the room. James's story has put everyone on edge.

"I think Gary's barmy going around that bird's gaff now and it's in the woods. To be fair, though, she is fit," remarks Tommy, nervously laughing.

"She ain't all that!" Ernie states. "And she's got funny burn-like marks on her face... err, horrible."

"I saw her in the shop the other day," Sara informs. "She is very attractive, but she didn't have any burn marks. In fact, one of the things I noticed was how clear her skin was."

Tommy jumps up, his face a sudden mask of worry.

"Sara, when did you see her?"

"Monday. I popped into the shop and bought some deodorant."

"Ernie, when did you first see her?"

Ernie looks at Tommy and frowns.

"Wednesday, why?"

Tommy nervously rubs his chin.

"So, Sara sees her Monday and she has no marks on her face, Ernie sees her Wednesday and there's burn-type marks on her boat! And Tuesday night you dump acid like poo on the face of the werewolf... don't you see what this could mean?"

Everyone apart from James looks blankly at him.

"It's like in the story James just told us. The werewolf's paw, the woman's hand... the werewolf's face the face, of Deloris!"

Sara and Scarlett gasp... to be fair, so do Chris and Len.

"I'm going to check on him." Tommy rushes from the room.

"Hang on, wait, me and Ernie are coming too. Len, you and Chris stay with the ladies."

Gary is in bits.

He finishes his dinner and laughs again.

"You really scared the crap out of me earlier, jumping me from behind like that," he chuckles and leans back in his chair.

Deloris smiles and touches her face.

"Does it still hurt?"

"No, just hate the bloody marks they left. Hopefully be gone completely soon. Teach me to stand to close to a spitting frying pan."

There is a moment of small talk and well, let's be honest, Gary wants to jump her and she's more than up for it.

He gets up, she whips her dress completely off and runs out naked into the night. There's no other way to say it, she actually does do that. One minute she's probing her boat, the next she's got her kit, all be it a single dress, off and is running about starkers.

Gary's eyes pop from his head. He follows and there in the moonlight, with arms outstretched, stands Deloris.

"I want to do it out here, in the open," she commands.

Gary is just about to jump her bones when he remembers the werewolf thing.

"Hang on, babe. We might be better off indoors. Keep it to yourself but I think there's a monster on the loose."

Deloris lowers her head, looks at him and bursts out laughing.

"Don't talk nonsense, they're just stories," she giggles and makes a mock howling noise.

She is taken quick and hard from behind… trust me, it ain't Gary. He just stands and watches as Deloris hits the dirt with Tommy Harris mounted on top off her.

"She's howling, Ernie," shouts James. "Take ya boot off and belt her with it."

Ernie removes his shoe. The clod-hopper is inches away from Deloris's head when Gary tackles him to the ground.

"What you doing, you bunch of twats," he roars. He manages to wrestle the boot off Ernie then drops it as he gets a whiff of Ernie's shoe odour!

Deloris begins to scream and swear. James pauses and scratches his head. Tommy just sits there not really knowing what to do next. Somehow, he realizes, his hand is resting somewhere it should not be and he quickly removes it.

"Pervert," she hisses at him.

Chris, Len and the women jump as the door crashes open.

Beckett shouts down about the noise and James apologises.

"You're alive," gasps Chris.

"Of course, I'm bloody alive, you dippy-looking sod," snaps Gary as he grabs the entire bottle of whiskey.

James and Tommy sheepishly walk in. Ernie has a wide grin spread across his face.

"What happened?" Sara asks.

Ernie's eyebrow raises multiple times and his grin widens even more.

"I saw her boobies... and Tommy got a fistfull of fur!"

So, James explains to all the series of unfortunate events and the demise of Gary's relationship with Deloris.

"Oh my god, the poor girl. How was she when you left her?" Sara asks concernedly.

"Not happy. We were lucky she didn't get the old bill. She was proper pissed off," Tommy states, draining his third beer in fifteen minutes.

"Nice arse, though."

Everyone looks at Ernie. Gary removes his trainer and before anyone can stop him, Ernie is hit with a size nine Nike blue stripe.

Earlier, it watches the turn of events from outside the cabin of Deloris.

Its mind, though splintered, remains and refrains from letting loose and tearing them all apart.

It moves further and deeper into the forest, running comically and insanely towards an opening an opening; that leads into an underground cave, its walls thick slabs of mud.

The girl, the hitchhiker, lays unconscious, tied and gaged. Her eyes suddenly flicker open upon the beast's arrival.

It walks slowly towards her. Her eyes, wide with fear and disbelief, look upon it.

It stops and hunches inches from her. She can see the face of the man that picked her up along the road buried beneath the hair, then the face is gone as a muzzle draws out, bones crack and teeth grow, blood and drool spill onto the ground.

It reaches out and places a clawed finger on her face. It tries to speak, and she hears words awkwardly spoken from its inhuman mouth.

The pure fear and madness of the event makes her want to pass out. She starts to feel dizzy but is brought back as its nail pushes into her cheek.

It laughs. Tears roll from her eyes and blood from her face. It screams and with lightning speed lunges its jaws towards her face. She waits but the werewolf's jaws halt less than an inch from her throat.

It stands back up and looks down; a clown-like grin appears and its muzzle seems to withdraw back into a human mouth.

"Look at what I am, my big ears, my big eyes… TEETH," it screams the word teeth and the muzzle explodes back out.

It leaps up into the air and lands upon her, knocking the wind out of her and breaking her ribs. She wriggles in pain and gags for air. Suffocating and in agony, it bites her face completely off… darkness, death… the beast feasts, it devours her flesh and laps at her blood.

Chapter Ten

Heath dresses and leaves Deloris's cabin; Gary's loss was his gain. He walks towards the village, jumps in his tractor and heads off to the farm. He'll settle scores with those cockney bastards later.

James opens his holdall Head bag. He looks across to see Ernie is still asleep.

Digging deeper into the bag he pulls out the object he is searching for. He holds the gun in his hand and grabs the small bullet case. He knows what to do or at least to begin with, but to capture the thing or to even find it is going to be a different ball game. Time is running out and he needs a plan. Unbeknown to him, a chain of events will speed things up but that is to happen later in the day. Ernie farts loudly. James slings the gun back inside the bag and leaves the room.

Scarlett pulls on her high-waisted jeans; her wrist bangles clatter together, she flicks on the radio to flop back on the bed and think of the situation she is in.

Mel and Kim are beginning to "Get Fresh for The Weekend"!

From in the bathroom, Sara sings along to the tune.

Beckett leaves the Tavern. Another meeting has been called; dark talk in dark times.

He awakens naked in the cave/den, bones stripped of flesh and blood-covered hands. A memory of last night draws on a surge of excitement as he gazes upon the remains of his victim. Let's move on from the depraved actions of a truly sick and evil individual.

Gary gives the breakfast a miss and sits sulking in the garden. It's 9.25 am and he ponders about going to the shop, maybe he could straighten things out with Deloris. Then Len appears, and he thinks again. When he gets back he's going to see Becky, apologise and see if he can grow up. He's obviously said this out loud as Len pats him on the shoulder and offers him a fag!

Scarlett brings him out a cup of tea and Sara suggests they have a nice quiet morning and then perhaps a good old pub lunch in the tavern and then get together and think of a way to capture the werewolf.

Gary begins to grin. At last, someone wants to offer some help and the idea of that encourages and brightens his mood and frame of mind. He leaps up and gives Sara a massive kiss on the cheek. He takes her by the hand and pulls her towards Chris, who is eating his third round of lime marmalade and toast.

"You got a blinding bird here you have (av)." Sara giggles and Chris looks up as Gary plucks the toast from his hand.

He rushes back into the garden, grabs his tea, kisses both Scarlett and Len and then runs upstairs to his room. They hear Tommy scream and curse.

"Gary's change of mood means, from experience, one thing! Some poor sod's going to suffer."

They all look at Chris and laugh.

So, the morning passes and the afternoon begins, they head to the tavern and have a lovely pub lunch. James returns to the Black Crow and a while later returns to the pub. They share jokes and talk about life in general then suddenly the tavern door opens and the mood changes.

Heath strides in accompanied by three heavy-set lads. They lean on the bar, order their drinks and stare across at the others.

"That's the bloke who was having a go at me the other afternoon," whispers Ernie.

"You got something to say?" Heath shouts across.

"No, mate. Were talking about ya, not to ya," Gary shouts back.

There's an uneasy silence.

"Maybe you attacking my woman is my (moi) business."

Gary gets up and walks towards him. Tommy and James follow.

"Your woman, mate! Funny, she never mentioned you last night."

Heath pushes himself off the bar. He towers over the others and grins.

"No, but she did mention what you did to her this morning," he growls and his face twists in anger.

There's no point in explanation; it's going to kick off whatever is said… get in first and get in fast!

Gary draws back and throws a punch. Unfortunately, he elbows Tommy and knocks his glasses off. Tommy, blind as a bat, scrambles to look for them as one of Heath's friends attacks James. Gary's fist connects with Heath's jaw but it's lost its power due to him hitting Tommy's chin.

Chris gets Sara and Scarlett out of the tavern and to do himself justice, returns only to see Gary Taylor fly and land on the table where Len and Ernie sit.

Heath charges towards the fallen Gary.

James has dispatched the farmhand who attacked him with a swift knee to the nuts and is now wrestling with another one.

Tommy is still on his knees looking for his glasses; the third farmhand knees him in the side of the face and Tommy falls sideways.

Chris fights with Len for cover under the table as Ernie rushes towards Tommy's attacker.

Meanwhile, Heath has Gary by the scruff of his brand-new Pringle and drags him up in the air. There is a loud rip and an even louder shout as Gary realises that it's ruined.

Tommy, on his knees now, grabs a stool and blindly swings it. Unfortunately, it catches Ernie in the kneecap.

"KNEE, KNEE, KNEE, OH, ME KNEE!" He screams and hops about, still repeatedly shouting KNEE!

James is on top of his assailant and is punching him in the face, until Ernie crashes into him, but to be fair the bloke's had enough which is just as well thanks to Ernie's involvement.

Gary is thrown across the room and lands against the remaining member of Heath's mob.

Gary jumps up grabs his ears and nuts him straight in the face, happy to see his nose explode. Tommy, meanwhile, has found his goggles and is up and ready.

Heath roars and charges forwards. Tommy steps in and plants a right cross straight on his chin. Heath is out cold before he hits the deck.

Chris and Len survey the situation and get up from under the table as the ladies walk back in.

The locals look on as the London boys stand, victorious, and Chris tells the women not to fear as everything is under control.

James pushes Ernie off him… Ernie shouts out KNEE!

Before anything else is said, the door opens and in walks the policeman from the other afternoon.

He looks around; Heath and his friends begin to move.

Wilks comes around from behind the bar and begins to explain.

"It's OK. I'll take it from here," the policeman, or PC Tristan Bates as he's known, cuts in.

He tells Gary and the others to wait outside. He bends down and assists Heath and his cronies to their feet.

"Right, I suggest you lads bugger off before you're nicked and sent down to Wexford for the evening."

Heath and co mutter and nurse their wounds; they leave by the far door off the tavern.

Bates explains to Wilks he'll ensure any damages incurred will be paid for by the London lads and leaves.

"I'll take them to the station and deal with them there."

Wilks nods and someone shouts that it was the other lads who started it.

"I'll take that in mind," replies Bates as he leaves.

They stand together, lined up like a rogue's gallery. Len notices Heath and his friends skulking away in the distance and shouts a warning.

"Yeah, that's it, go while you can." His voice breaks half way through and Scarlett nudges him.

"You the ring leader, are you?" barks Bates.

Len says nothing and points to Chris.

"Thought as much," growls the policeman grabbing the open-mouthed Murren by his collar.

"Think you had all better follow me." He pushes the bewildered Chris in front of him and beckons the rest to follow. They walk along the village with their heads slightly hung low. Curtains twitch and tongues from the village women halt as the villainous parade marches along.

They troop around the back of some houses and turn into a small alley… and as if by magic a cottage-type house with a sign indicating Police detachedly sits.

"Blimey, who shrunk Scotland Yard?" jokes Gary.

"Very funny, just get inside, you little Herbert," moans the disgruntled copper.

"Alright," Gary enters first, and the others follow.

The inside of the so-called Police station is very different to any nick Gary Taylor has ever frequented.

A large desk is the first thing they notice. On it sits a small filing tray and a phone. There is also a small radio set playing a Bangles tune very quietly.

Behind the desk to the left is a large leather sofa. Behind that, a door.

To the right there is a large open fireplace, a leather chair and a table with a lamp. Behind it, another door and a well-stocked book shelf.

The room itself was quite dim, its floors dark wood, its walls painted crimson red.

"In you all go," Bates motions as he proceeds to close the front door and flick the wireless off.

"Was enjoying that tune," Gary grins. "Manic Monday. More like a fudged-up Friday!"

"My knee hurts!" Ernie complains and he dumps himself into the chair.

Bates motions the others towards the sofa. Scarlett, Sara, Len and Chris sit and bunch together. Gary, Tommy and James stand behind it. Gary tries to sit on the arm but slips off and falls to the floor!

Bates sits in the chair behind the desk and swivels around to face them.

"Listen, Magnum! They bloody started it," Gary moans embarrassed by his mishap.

Bates leans forward in his chair and points the pen he holds towards the disgruntled Gary Taylor.

"You're not here because of what happened in the pub so calm down."

"Then what are we here for?" Sara enquires politely.

"Because you know, as I do, that Drarkland has a werewolf!"

The room falls silent and for a while there is an exchange of nervous looks, the policeman confirming what they suspect is like a punch to the stomach. Chris places a shaky arm around Sara, more for his own comfort as for hers. Len grasps Scarlett's hand and makes a funny squeak... Ernie points to his knee.

"And how are you aware of this?" James asks. "What makes you certain enough to bring us here and put a statement of such fantastical proportion to us!"

"Deloris told me what you lot said and did to her."

"Fair enough," James sniffs and looks sheepishly at the others.

"But how do you know that we are right and there is a werewolf on the loose?"

Bates looks towards the blond, thick-set man.

"Because I've seen it and because I know of the legends... and they're true, all of them."

"Can I smoke?" Gary says, shaking his cigarette packet.

"Yes, my boy(boi), you can and before I explain something to you, you're welcome to a drink. I think we can all do with one."

He opens the large bottom draw of his desk and produces a large bottle of whiskey and plastic cups.

Everyone accepts, even the ladies who don't even like the stuff. Bates pours away and begins.

"They settled in the village hundreds of years back; a family from France, their name was D'aramitz. They were rumoured to come from a small village in the French Pyrenees region. They arrived in the village, the husband and wife and five children. They had travelled from the coast on board a boat said to have been blighted by death... as was their village. Soon livestock was found slaughtered, then children in the village of Drarkland disappeared.

Then the secret of the D'aramitz family came to light... they were all werewolves! The villagers rounded them up during the daylight, tied them to a stake and burned them alive. They screamed and howled, changing from human to wolf form and back again. The D'aramitz family may have gone but the curse remained and from time to time manages to return and once again it has.

The werewolf is back amongst us!"

For a while no one says anything, then Gary pipes up.

"We capture this thing and were rich."

Bates laughs.

"And your plan is...?"

"Dunno', we're working on it."

Bates looks away from Gary and gazes out of the window.

"So why are you telling us all this?" James asks, coming around to the desk and pouring himself another drink.

"Because no one will do anything, and people will be killed. I don't fancy being supper for some crazed lycan! We capture this beast, we take it chained from here and we, as you say, get rich."

Scarlett looks at Sara. Shades of sympathy touch her face.

"This werewolf, it's still at times a human. Surely it needs help and understanding. I mean, if it's a curse it has no choice."

Bates nods and replies.

"It and he/she does need help, but we can't give it that help here. We get it to a place where it can be helped. Once I leave this village, trust me, I won't be returning, and if anyone finds out we are having this conversation none of us will be leaving."

"So, what's the plan, I take it you have one?"

Bates stands up and faces James.

"I've discovered its lair and it's there we'll wait for it. We'll await its arrival and shoot it."

"With silver bullets," James adds.

"No, silver will kill it permanently, as will fire, but normal bullets will kill the beast for twenty-four hours and then it will return to life but by then we will have it chained and be on our way out of here."

Bates opens the top draw of his desk and produces a revolver.

"None of you must speak of this to anyone in the village; our lives depend on our silence and cooperation with each other... here's the plan and what's to happen."

Bates pours everyone another drink and explains the plan; everyone feels the shadow of doom creep over them apart from Gary. Gary just thinks of all the money he's going to make and the film he'll direct... well, not so much him but Steve Spielberg or that Lucas bloke who done that dopey Star Wars film!

They leave the station/house of Bates and head back to the Black Crow. Their story simple and straightforward should anyone ask... cautioned for disrupting the peace. Bates watches them go and sits in the leather armchair. He holds his glass of whiskey and takes a large glug. Downwardly wiping his moustache he releases a sigh and closes his eyes.

So, the motley crew head back, all in their own thoughts but pretty much thoughts united... what a week! Chris and Len find love and they all discover a werewolf roams the forest, To be honest, I don't know which is more surprising... or horrific!

Chris stops, as does the rattling buckles on his sandals, and looks at his friends.

"How about we drive into to Wexted for dinner and a drink?"

"In other words, let's get out of Dodge for a bit," laughs Tommy.

"Precisely," Chris agrees.

"I'll drive," Scarlett offers. "Night off for you, sweetie."

Sara smiles and takes Chris's hand.

"I take it you two lemons are going in the love bug," jokes Garry, indicating towards Len and Chris.

"I'll take you lot in the Capri," says James. He stares at Ernie. "But you aint having no ruby's tonight (curry)," he warns.

Ernie's face creases and his lips puff out.

"Wasn't going to have a curry, ya bloody know -all," he miserably retorts.

They continue with their trot to the Black Crow and ready themselves.

The wireless blasts in Gary's and Tommy's room. "Ghostbusters," it plays.

Mandate aftershave is poured, gel is splodged, and a selection of expensive tennis wear is chosen, both men sporting a tiny crocodile on their left tit.

For James and Ernie, Van Halen is continually shouting he's going to jump... until James turns his tape deck off.

Ernie, who is busy insulting the porcelain, shouts to turn it on. James ignores him and selects a clean white shirt to go with his navy sports jacket and black Farrah slacks.

Chris is bare chested in the bathroom, shaving and humming "Who's afraid of the big bad wolf". Len's humour is diverted from Chris's belly hanging over his shorts to the fact that tomorrow they might all be eaten. He plucks his spikey mullet up and fiddles with his camera.

Sara and Scarlett sit and talk quietly; they are scared and don't know what to do. Something fantastically impossible has become a reality and now things seem much darker and if things couldn't get worse, they can hear Ernie in the next room, making odd noises in his bathroom.

Beckett, who has been creeping around the landing and standing outside the ladies' bedroom door, slopes off.

He treads gently down the stairs and once at the bottom turns into the kitchen.

Beckett opens the cupboard and grabs a large glass. Opening the fridge, he withdraws an even larger bottle of strong Scrumpy and sits down at the small wooden table, pouring himself a drink and downing the entire contents. He thinks of the village, the damned curse and the fate of those in it.

Sara and Scarlett enter the lounge; the lads are already there waiting. Sara smiles at Chris; how lovely he looks dressed in his Hawaiian shirt and cream slacks. Len gazes at Scarlett and his heart thumps; she is simply stunning, her damp hair lays against tanned shoulders. She wears an off-the-shoulder denim top and denim pedal pushers... how did I pull that, he thinks.

"How did you pull that?" Ernie bleats.

There is a chorus of soft laughter amongst the men, apart from Len, and Sara indicates for them to perhaps leave for Wexted.

Sara is wearing a bright yellow dress; Gary thinks she looks like a fat canary.

They leave the Black Crow and jump in the cars. From the kitchen window, Beckett watches them drive away. He pours another drink as James Austin switches on his car radio. Beckett sits back down, and Bow Wow Wow go Wild in the Country.

They arrive at Wexted and park up (I've given you the layout earlier so let's move on).

The Windmill was about as trendy a pub as they were going to find. The lights were flicking softly from blue to red to yellow and there were gleaming silver barstools and bright green plastic tables.

Upstairs was a dance floor and from it Altered Images song Happy Birthday.

"Shit song," Ernie moans, pushing a small bloke out the way to get to the bar.

Chris performs a quick dance to the tune and Gary clocks a blond sort squeezed tightly into a boob tube, her lips plastered with pink lipstick and a cigarette hanging from her gob, remind him of home.

"Couple in here and then we can go for something to eat," suggests Len.

"Yeah, and then back here for the disco," Tommy says as he dances next to Chris.

"Sounds good to me," giggles Scarlett and grabs Sara's hand.

"We're off to powder our noses," laughs Sara. "Large gin and tonic for me please, Chris."

"And a coke with ice for me," shouts Scarlett over her shoulder as they march off.

Chris waves and moves to the bar.

"Them girls are shit scared, you know that? They're proper putting on a brave face," Tommy announces to the others at the bar.

"I know," agrees Gary. "That's why they aint coming tomorrow."

"How do you mean?" asks James.

"Like I said, their gonna stay in the B&B while we go with Bates." He looks at Len and Chris. "And you two are going to stay with them."

"But Bates said were all to meet," moans Ernie.

"I don't care what he says. I aint taking two birds on a werewolf hunt. They could end up brown bread, son, and Gary Taylor does not, I repeat does not, get women killed."

"So how comes them two goons get to stay with them?" Tommy asks.

"Cause they aint no use to us in the battlefield, mate. Not only that, they're their birds and last line of defence, god help them! If anything should happen to us, you two turnips have got to get them girls out of there and get some help."

"Dunno whether to be happy or insulted," squeaks Len.

Len, for no reason, falls forward and bumps into Ernie. Ernie pushes him back and he bounces off Tommy. This has no bearing on this story, but it just happened like that.

View to a kill comes on by Duran Duran and Ernie grumbles. "Another shit song!"

So, the ladies return, and Gary explains the new plan. Sara and Scarlett are relieved and both hug the now smug-looking Gary Taylor. Len looks on angrily, shocked as Gary pretends to grab Scarlett's arse and over her shoulder Gary pouts his lips and grins at him. They all have some more drinks then head to a local Chinese restaurant.

A few sweet 'n' sour dishes later and they're back in the Windmill. They go up to the disco and crack on. Chris and Len dance with Sara and Scarlett to a Madonna track. Gary, without Len knowing, disappears with the blond sort in the boob tube. He classily takes her into the disabled toilet and reappears five minutes later, though he'll tell you it was ten (we will touch on this romantic moment later) and Tommy and James discuss tomorrow's plans.

Ernie is at a table talking to some girl dressed up in punk gear. She's from Croydon and on holiday with her mum. She tells him her name is Candy and she takes his number, telling him she'll bell him next week sometime. Ernie nods, holds in a fart and awkwardly kisses her goodbye. They enjoy the night and leave without any trouble.

Candy walks back to her hotel room; her elderly mum holds her arm.

"Who was that big galoot with crispy seaweed stuck in his stubble?" she asks.

"He's no galoot mum, he's a Hells Angel and a drummer in a band and tomorrow he's off to catch a werewolf."

As they walk up the stairs to their hotel her mum chuckles.

"Catch a werewolf. Daft looking sod probably couldn't catch a cold."

Chapter Eleven
Saturday

Even a man who is pure in heart and says his prayers by night,
May become a wolf when the wolf bane blooms and the
autumn moon is bright.

The body lay still, the smell of rot and filth seeped from its pores.

Hair grew black and patchy from its body, eyes still closed. Its head turns, the remains of last night's feed nest in its lips and on its chin.

It opens its mouth and releases a howl.

Eyes open wide, it suddenly leaps to its feet and searches around its environment; it sees what it needs and lunges towards its haven.

"Make sure you bloody spray it in there after," shouts James from his bed. "Told you not to have extra chilli sauce on that kebab last night. You're a greedy git, you really bloody are."

Ernie ignores and continues with his mission. He slams the toilet door and then slams his arse on the bog! He releases a sudden cry of pain.

James gets up and smiles.

"That chilli sauce burning your arse, is it?"

"No! I must have some left on me fingers! I've just picked me nose and burnt me nostril."

James smiles once again and shakes his head.

"And I gave up a room with a beautiful, intelligent, leggy blond for this!"

Tommy sits on the end of his bed. Gary is still sleeping; evidence in the way of his snoring is a giveaway.

He thinks about the situation and what the day has in store; they meet Bates at the edge of the forest at seven tonight and head towards a werewolf's hide out and there they wait until it arrives. They shoot the furry bastard, chain it up and bundle it into the back of Bates's police wagon… the rest, if they live to see the rest, is down to Gary and his knack of making dosh.

Tommy scratches his head and wonders how it will pan out… he walks over and twats Gary across the forehead. A smile of satisfaction spreads across his face as Gary lets out a howl of pain.

"What d'you do that for, ya four-eyed git?"

"For selling me shit aftershave sixteen years ago, you slag!"

Chris and Len are already up, washed and dressed as are Sara and Scarlett.

They sit in the room of the women and discus werewolves, breakfast and the shocking revelation that Chris and Gary are family.

"How?" Sara asks chuckling.

"His old fella and Chris's old dear are brother and sister," Len informs them.

Chris shoots Len a pained glance.

"Yes, thank you, Lennard, but I am quite capable of explaining my family tree to the ladies," Chris snaps.

Chris gets ready to explain when Len decides to fiddle with the girl's radio, turning the volume up full blast to the sound of Dexy's Midnight Runners.

"Toodle langa langa Toodle langa fang…"

Chris jumps and nearly falls of the edge of the bed. He snatches the radio and jams the volume down.

"Isn't it bad enough we might be devoured by a blood-thirsty creature from hell! The last thing I need is you blasting out Jackie Wilson Said!"

Len apologises, Sara takes Chris's hand, Scarlett bites hard on her lip trying hard not to laugh.

In the Tavern, Wilks sits and talks with Beckett.

Later in the morning, Sara and Scarlett get provisions from the store, cigarettes and such, nothing is said much between them and Deloris, basic forced pleasantries and some frosted glances is all.

For lunch they all head to the Tavern. Apologies are made, and Wilks is kind enough to point out that it was the village lads that started the ruckus and not them. There is no sign of Heath or his cronies and though Wilks seems happy to have them in his pub, they can't help but feel that all eyes are watching them with some level of suspicion.

So, the day goes by. They eat, drink and converse as normally as possible but always with one eye on the clock and soon the time comes when they have to leave the sanctuary of the village boozer and head back to the Black Crow for their evening of fearful adventure. Ozzy Osbourne aptly sings "Bark At The Moon" on the juke box as Ernie downs his pint and belches loudly.

Bates leaves the station and looks around. He senses someone is watching but continues to the meeting point.

Gary tells Chris to take Len and the girls to their room and keep an eye out. He gathers the lads and then awaits James who's still in his room.

"Come on," Gary hisses as his friend comes down the stairs. "It's nearly seven."

James waves him away and they leave. Beckett spies from the crack in the kitchen door.

The remaining four are sat in Len and Chris's room; they watch as Gary and the others walk towards the woods, their shadows growing longer as the night starts to close in. As I said earlier, night comes quicker in the country!

Think I did anyway.

Scarlett turns the radio on to take the fearful edge out of the room's atmosphere and glances once again out into the night. Duran Duran sing about the "Wild Boys!" ...right now, those bunch of heroes are her Wild Boys.

"Evening lads," Bates evenly greets them as he steps from the trees.

"You got your gun?" Tommy asks. Bates pats his side.

"Got mine, too," James mentions.

There is a look of surprise amongst his friends.

"Where did you get a gun from?" Gary asks, shocked.

"Never you mind," James replies.

Bates looks at him, open mouthed.

"You got a firearm? Hope you got a license for that, my lad."

James frowns.

"Look, you burk, we're going on a werewolf hunt. The last thing you want to worry about is me having a bleedin' gun license."

Bates thinks about it and nods.

"Good point. OK, lads, let's do this. Follow me and be silent."

So, they do. They walk further into the forest and after a while Tommy and Bates turn on their torches; the night is drawing in.

They follow Bates into a clearing; three tree stumps stand in a circle and the forest floor starts to slope down. They continue.

Moments later they stop. Bates indicates to a large bush. Following him, he halts and pushes the leaves to one side.

"It's in here," he whispers. "Follow me and keep quiet."

The first thing they notice is the smell. God, it's horrific. Rot, decay and something else… death.

"I know, lads, it's awful but try and bear it. We need to get deeper inside so when it turns up we are ready."

"What about the chains and stuff?" Ernie panics.

"I stashed them here earlier," Bates answers.

As they walk deeper into the den, the smell grows stronger, almost unbearable.

"Stone me, how much further? The stink is making me gag," Gary hisses.

Bates stops, he flicks his torch back towards them.

"Hush, I hear something." He moves past them and almost protectively stands in front of the last man, Ernie. He faces towards the den's entrance.

"It's here!," he silently warns.

There is a cold silence. Gary begins to think this might be a bad idea.

"W-where?" Ernie nervously asks, his legs turning to jelly.

"HERE."

The word "here" was more of a comical scream than a shout, but as it dashes from Bates's lips there is nothing comical about his face.

His mouth is twisted into a twisted grin, teeth jut from the side, sharp and uneven.

Within seconds his height increases, clothes rip and tear.

Tommy keeps the torch shinning at the thing that was once Bates. The others stare in horrific fascination.

His brow widens and lowers, bones break and crackle as skin splits and fur blossoms.

"I'm going to devour you all and then I'm going to rip the other four to ribbons." His voice deepens and becomes gruff, spittle flies and his tongue lolls forward.

James draws his revolver and takes aim.

"Not if I can help it."

The laugh that leaves Bates's mouth turns into a howl.

"Bullets won't do nothing. I lied, dummy, only fire and silver." Bates is now more wolf than human, and his words sound awkward as his mouth becomes a muzzle.

"That's why I got a silver bullet in the gun… dummy! Keep the torch on him, Tommy."

Bates looks upon him with complete hatred and a hint of fear.

A guttural roar is released. The werewolf leaps forward. James pulls the trigger.

Everyone, bar James and the beast, wince at the explosion and drop to their knees.

The bullet hits the side of its head as darkness hits the den, due to Tommy the tit dropping the torch.

There is a scream of agony. Tommy scrambles and lifts the torch. He points it towards the hunched creature that has now scampered past them back into the den.

The bullet, although hitting its head, has passed through flesh and worked itself out. However, damage has been done and what they see before them is the freakish result.

The body is still that of the werewolf, but the head has changed back to that of Bates, though a few fangs remain and one wolfish ear.

"Bloody hell, you're ugly," comments Gary.

Bates curses and screams.

"Damn you, your mothers are whores to bastards," he screeches.

"Tell us something we don't know, mate," grunts Tommy.

James fires off another shot. The bullet hits Bates in the chest… nothing happens.

"Only had one silver one. Melted my saint Christopher into the bullet, the rest are normal."

"Aw, bollocks," Tommy moans.

Bates begins to rise from his squatting position, his face morphing back into that of the wolf's.

"Shit, were done for," Gary shouts.

Ernie pushes past and for once the Hells Angel that he isn't, comes to the surface.

"Ernie, NO!" Gary cries but it's too late. They watch as he strides forwards.

The howl the creature releases is one of pure agony as Ernie's boot connects with its dangling wolfish testicles.

It falls back. Ernie leaps upon it and lifts it by its fur; slamming it against the wall, he stamps on its foot and punches its nose... the others watch open mouthed and amazed... Ernie "Oddbod" Smith is bashing up a werewolf!

Then it all goes wrong.

The werewolf grabs and throws Ernie. He flies along and crashes into his pals. Once again they are plunged into semi-darkness.

Tommy again fumbles for the torch. He shines it but now the beast has leaped past them and is heading for the den's entrance. It turns and almost smiles and then it dawns upon them as to where it is heading to... the Black Crow!

It bounds forwards, towards the forest and easier prey.

"Wonder how they're getting on?" asks Len, looking out of the window. The night has come, and he can't see a thing.

"Dunno," shrugs Chris, his face a mask of worriment and concern.

"God, I hope they're OK," Sara blurts as she begins to cry.

Chris places an arm around her shoulders and comforts her; Scarlett does the same for Len.

The beast collapses, the silver bullet though not powerful enough a shot to kill, has caused some damage and trauma. Its legs give way and it crashes to the forest floor. Once again, Bates's face is forming, and he screams in pain and in hate.

They run from the den and out into the forest. To be honest, none of them have a bloody clue how to get back to the rest, none of them apart from Tommy.

"Because I'm a cab driver, remembering directions are my bread and butter."

"Great, but you're also the slowest," shouts Gary.

"Belt up and follow me."

The pain that sears through its head passes and once again the werewolf is on its hind legs; it howls into the night and races on.

"Mother of god!" The words silently leave Scarlett's lips. Len pulls away from her embrace and looks up.

"They've been slain," he squeals.

Chris jumps up. Terrified he paces the room.

"Now we don't know that," his voice was breaking.

"Turn the lamp off," Sara shouts.

"WHY?" Chris yells, panic taking over.

"So we can see better outside," Sara explains.

"Good idea," agrees Scarlett as she flicks the switch off.

The room is plunged into sudden darkness. They sit still and let their eyes adjust, Then they all move and look towards the forest.

"How far now?" Gary breathlessly cries.

"Not much further," Tommy breathlessly replies.

It bursts from the forest. The moon shines upon it and Chris, upon spotting it, nearly faints.

The women and Len scream; panic takes over.

"The door," Chris shouts as he grabs the mattress.

Len rushes to help him and they begin to form a barricade.

The werewolf stops. It has reached the Black Crow and it begins to sniff, for its prey are here. Dropping to all fours it releases a long low snarl.

"We're nearly out the woods." Tommy's words spur them on.

"It's outside the front door, I can hear it." Sara's words chill them to the bone.

It returns to its hind legs and smashes the door to the Black Crow open; wood shatters and splinters. Beckett is nowhere to be seen but it knows where the others hide.

Once again, it falls to all fours and begins to climb the stairs.

As Tommy leads his friends from the forest into the clearing, Len thinks of his son and decides if he's going to die, he'll die a hero and not a coward... Len Jnr's dad will not die a coward!

"Sara, Scarlett, get into the wardrobe... me and Chris will hold it off," he orders, his usual high-pitched voice taking on a deeper brogue.

It prowls along the corridor and stops directly at their room. It hears them, and they hear it, apart from the two woman who are bundled in the wardrobe.

"SHIT!" shouts Gary as he sees the front door smashed to pieces.

The barricade they made does nothing to hold the beast. To be precise, the door opens outwards, so it simply opens it and looks in... it sees the two men though it senses two females as well.

Chris and Len look upon the nightmarish form that stands before them and freeze.

Tommy is the first one in, Gary close behind. James draws his gun, even though it can't hurt the monster and Ernie behind him picks up a piece of timber from the broken door.

As they reach the bottom of the stairs, the werewolf leaps into the room; teeth and claws flash.

Len is the first to respond as he grabs Chris's suitcase and hits it across the head. The beast does not break stride and simply knocks him across the room.

Chris falls back on the bed and comically bounces back up. He clashes into the werewolf and they both spin sideways. To be honest, and I know this is supposed to be a serious part of the story but it was bloody funny watching a scared beyond belief chubby bloke and a snarling werewolf collide like so!

Tommy and the others reach the top of the stairs; they have no plan of saving attack only loyalty to aid their friends.

Chris looks up from where he lays and sees the werewolf lunging towards him. He knows it's over but before he gets to meet his maker he hears one last battle cry and that battle cry comes from a very unexpected source.

"SAY GIT!"

Tommy and the other lads race into the room. Jumping over mattresses and bedside tables, they charge... apart from Ernie who trips and stacks it onto the floor!

They all hear the same words as Chris and they all see, apart from the two women and the fallen Ernie, Len as he swings his camera towards the beast's head. Wielding it like Excalibur, it connects with its face, jams in its jaws and is sent operational by one of its fangs.

...There is a sudden silence, a blinding flash and a bloody great explosion.

Tommy, Gary and James dive for cover, Ernie stays where he lies, as does Chris... the werewolf's head bursts into flames.

The force of the bang sends it and its fiery face sailing across the bedroom. In pain beyond belief, it leaps to its feet and howls, screams and cries... they all look on. Sara and Scarlett peak from the cupboard and witness as it dances in pain.

The fire spreads along its fur, consuming its entire body. With one lasting look, its eyes shine through the flames and gaze upon them with cruel damnation. It falls backwards. It releases a loud, soul-bending howl.

The descent from the bedroom window takes place and the thud can be heard as it slams against the concrete ground.

By the time they reach the body, the flames have somehow died out.

The body, though chard, is recognisable as Bates; all traces of the wolf are gone.

"Len, you bastard, you've vaporised him!" screams Gary, pound signs disappearing.

"No, I ain't. You can still recognise him," Len protests.

"It's hardly a passport picture," moans Tommy.

"Yes and even if it was, what we got? I'll tell you what we got. The dead body of some mustachoid git," James informs them.

"Correct lads... a dead policeman."

In unison, they all turn to see where the voice has come from.

Beckett, Wilks and three other villagers all holding rifles stand staring at them. Gary gets the feeling that this is about to go tits up!

"We acted in self-defence," Chris begins to explain but is silenced by Wilks waving his hand.

"Don't need any explanations from any of you. You're all outsiders and aren't to blame for what's happened here."

"So, you ain't going to shoot us?" Len nervously asks.

"No," Wilks replies. "If anyone's to blame, it's us for not warning you and Beckett for inviting outsiders into our village."

"I didn't invite them," Beckett sadly protests.

"Encouraging them by opening a blooming B&B then," Wilks snaps.

Beckett lowers his head.

They all turn and look at the body. A wind picks up and suddenly it starts to flake and spill into the night, pieces of ash are carried upwards and away until there is nothing left. The wind dies down. A soft distant howl plays from somewhere in the forest… or maybe it's just the wind.

You may have expected a more epic battle! Perhaps one of our hapless heroes getting ripped to pieces! But I can't write what didn't happen. The beast had its time and the reign of this one was short but brutal. I think although Bates was a policeman he was also a mean and nasty person deep down. He enjoyed the killing for the killing. He thrilled when remembering what he had done to his victims. Though one was deserved, the others were not, and the line between killing as a demonic, slavering monster with no control and the perverse pleasure that those memories bring afterwards is a big difference. Others from the past hated and felt remorse over their actions as a werewolf; Bates, however, did not.

They leave in the morning.

Nothing is said as they go. There really is nothing to say anyway.

They promise never to return and to say nothing to anyone. The villagers watch as they drive through and out of the village, Wilks steps from the tavern and lifts a hand to wave goodbye.

From the general store, Deloris stands alone, her eyes fixed on Gary, a sad smile of what might have been hangs on her lips… well, she's only human, Gary smugly thinks. Deloris turns and rushes back inside. Gary thinks it's because she's heartbroken… truth be told, she's happy to see the back of him. The sad smile is a horrid case of constipation and the sudden rush inside is the realisation the laxative tabs have started to work.

As the cars drive out of the village the morning begins to darken, the clouds become grey and the sun hides behind them. A crack of thunder crashes out followed by a dash of lightning and heavy rain. What an apt way to leave Drarkland.

Well, what do you think? Not a bad story, aye?

Let's move on a bit.

They all get home. Gary gets back in with Becky. He has been saving all the money he's been making on the videos for Len to take his son away on holiday.

He hands it over and Len feels himself well-up. Gary, though a pain in the bum most of the time, is a truly good friend and on hearing this, Becky rushes back into his arms, forgiving him for his stupid ways and loving him more for helping her brother.

Chris and Sara have fallen deeply in love and it's not long before Sara moves in. Chris now has someone to help fill up his double bed and his life.

Scarlett and Len also get a place together. They rent a beautiful flat around the corner from Chris and go on holiday to Spain with Len Jnr happily in tow. Keith seems to be more accommodating and understanding towards Len, probably because Tommy and Gary grabbed him outside the local Chinese one night and had a quite word in his shell-like!

Tommy and Jane get married and have a fantastic wedding Gary, the best man, buys them a wedding gift that they see a few weeks later being shown on the TV show Police Five (an old-fashioned version of Crime Watch). They have a wonderful honeymoon in a small Spanish Island.

James inherits a fortune from a rich aunt. He leaves his job and opens his own paranormal investigation business called Austin Investigations. He moves back to the manor and buys a nice five-bedroom drum with his new girlfriend and co-investigator, Sky Sinclair. Yep, they met up and totally hit it off.

Ernie gets a phone call from the bird he met on holiday. To his surprise and the others, she does like him. Turns out she's a singer and is putting a band together. She needs a drummer and Ernie jumps on board… the heavy rock-punk band "Werewolf Candy" is born… Ernie also gets his card stamped and moves her into his parents' house.

So, they may not have become rich (apart from James) and famous, but things worked out OK. In fact, you could say that the summer of '85 was in fact the summer of love for them all.

The village of Drarkland is never mentioned to anyone outside their group and to this day remains a village where outsiders never venture simply because not many people know of it, though I have visited it from time to time to see if anything has changed…to see if anything has returned.

The End… for now!

I would like the reader to play the song "Loves Great Adventure" by Ultravox for effect.

WAIT… It's not quite over!

Remember earlier in the story at the Windmill in Wexted… The Romantic Moment!

Gary takes the blond sort by the hand and drags her into the disabled toilet. He pounces upon her, shoving his tongue in her gob. She's game and grabs him roughly by the hair with one hand and squeezes his arse with the other. There's snogging and the sort is just about to exit her boob-tube when…!

"I can't do it, babe! I ain't gonna cheat on me bird, not while there's still a chance! Here's ten quid. Get yourself a drink and if anyone should ask, Gary Taylor gave you ten minutes of heaven!"

She looks at him and shrugs and leaves the bog… Loves Great Adventure!

The End… Again!